# MAITLAND

## UNDER SIEGE

# MAITLAND
## UNDER SIEGE

### JAMES PATRICK HUNT

Five Star • Waterville, Maine

First Edition
First Printing: April 2006

Published in 2006 in conjunction with
Tekno Books and Ed Gorman.

Set in 11 pt. Plantin.

Printed in the United States on permanent paper.

**Library of Congress Cataloging-in-Publication Data**

Hunt, James Patrick, 1964–
   Maitland under siege / by James Patrick Hunt.—1st ed.
      p. cm.
   ISBN 1-59414-440-0 (hc : alk. paper)
   1. Antique dealers—Fiction.  2. Bounty hunters—Fiction.
   3. Fugitives from justice—Fiction.  4. African American
   men—Fiction.  5. Chicago (Ill.)—Fiction.  I. Title.
PS3608.U577M358 2006
   813'.6—dc22                                    2005030119

For my mother

"All men can be criminals, if tempted; all men can be heroes, if inspired."

—G. K. Chesterton

# PART 1
## THE WEEK BEFORE

# ONE

When Dreamer said all they were going to do was just talk and get this shit down tight, Hicks knew he'd have to bring a gun. He'd known Dreamer since they were kids, little boys in South Chicago, and Dreamer had been a dumb shit and a bad liar even before he'd been a junkie. Not a bad man, really, just weak and stupid. Weak, mostly.

Thomas Hicks at that time was thirty years old. Tall and well built, no fat on him, but feeling ten years older on the inside. He'd been a member of the Parktown Crips when he was eleven or twelve—he couldn't remember which—got busted at twenty after sticking up a liquor store. Went in the state penitentiary on a three-to-five sentence. Friends of his had died while he served his sentence—one of them shot by a Vietnamese convenience store owner—and the irony of being safer in prison was not lost on him. Not that he liked prison. Prison was prison and anyone that tried to intellectualize the experience had never been there. He did his time—three years, eleven months—lifted weights, read a lot of books and magazines, didn't rape or get raped. He kept his mouth shut unless it was necessary to talk, but he didn't keep his head down because if you do that too much they'll think you're weak and come after you . . . quiet but not subdued, that was the key. He came out at the age of twenty-four and got a job driving a truck for a linen company and avoided friends of his that hadn't been killed or sent to prison. He worked eight to five, driving the truck and went home to an efficiency apartment that he kept clean. He stayed away from drugs and the old habits. He lived his life minimally, no cable television because he thought it was like a drug. Some people thought he was one of those homeboys who went to the joint and came out all weird, acting mystical and shit. But he had not gotten religion in prison. He had just learned to think and to think differently.

He was a good-looking guy. Women liked him and he liked them. Ultimately, it was that that set his life off the rails. Again. He was in a club, alone, and a tall sister came on to him. Calling him a handsome black man, *oooing* and *mmming* and so on, and he was enjoying it. And then her man came up, a young punk-ass, maybe twenty-two years old and decided to be offended about it.

Hicks took it in. The boy was a punk, but cowards are often more dangerous than brave men, particularly when they wanted to impress a woman who was probably wanting this scene all along. Hicks, the retired gangster, made eye contact with the punk and said, "Brother, I'm sorry. I didn't know she was your woman."

"You gonna be sorry, all right," the punk said.

Shit.

Hicks raised his hands in a conciliatory gesture, but he kept solid eye contact. Submissive, but just.

"Now, I said I was sorry," Hicks said. "But that's it."

The boy's carrying, Hicks thought. He could see it in the way the boy was starting to put his hand in his jacket, moving it in more now, and Hicks moved, quickly, his left hand grabbing the boy by the wrist, his right reaching into the boy's jacket and pulling out the gun inside. Then Hicks backhanded the boy across the face.

"Don't you ever pull a fucking gun on me boy. You hear."

Thomas slapped him again.

The boy's name was Jaron Nelson. If Hicks had known that, he wouldn't have slapped him. Well, wouldn't have slapped him the second time maybe. But it was easy to look back on things, harder to know what to do at the time.

There were tears in the boy's eyes now.

Hicks looked around the club. People were staring at him. Ten years ago he'd have bathed in it. Now he felt awful. Trapped. Again.

Hicks turned to the woman.

He said, "You happy now?"

"Fuck you," she said. "You ain't so cool."

Hicks walked out of the club. Half a block away he dumped the gun into a trash bin.

He felt the foreboding, unfamiliar and yet familiar. He knew, he just knew, that this would trigger something.

He was right. He slapped the man on Saturday. Monday afternoon, Dreamer Rasheed came up to him in a parking lot while Hicks was on the job.

Hicks was in uniform, khaki pants and a windbreaker that said "Mayfield Linen Service" on it.

"What do you want, Dreamer?"

"Man, I just need to talk to you."

"I'm working."

"I ride with you then."

"That's not allowed."

"It's important, Thomas."

Hicks looked around. There was no one there to see him, but two black men in the truck—one of them not in the uniform—would make the clientele and his employers nervous. It was what it was.

"Just for a little while, Dreamer."

Dreamer got in the large white van and Hicks started the drive to his next delivery.

11

"First of all," Dreamer said, "I'm here as a friend, you understand."

"Yeah? Whose friend?"

"Your friend, man." Dreamer tried to put some hurt into his voice.

"Who else's friend?"

"You know who Victor is?"

"Victor Nelson? Yeah, I heard of him."

"He's got a little brother, Jaron? You know him?"

"No."

"Well, you should. He the boy you bitch slapped at Orion's last weekend."

Hicks felt a thud in his heart. He maintained composure. "That right?"

"Yeah," Dreamer said. "That's right." He sounded a bit sad.

Hicks changed his tone slightly. He said, "He was going to shoot me, Dreamer."

"That's not what he say."

"I don't care what he say. I was there."

"Well . . ."

"Victor wants me dead now?"

"No, man, it ain't like that. He just wants to talk to you, you know. Get this shit down, tight."

"Get what down, tight?"

Dreamer made a pained expression.

Hicks said, "You tell Victor I never meant to diss him. Tell him I didn't know the boy was his brother. Just tell him that."

"Victor just wants it to be right, that's all."

"How he gonna make it right, Dreamer? By hiring a couple of men to cap me? Or have a couple of dudes beat me into a deep unconsciousness?"

"Thomas, you don't do this, they going to come after you. They can cap you anytime. You know how it is. Just meet with the man, then don't none of us have to worry about it anymore."

Hicks regarded Dreamer.

"You worried about it, Dreamer?"

Dreamer looked scared.

"I don't know," he said.

Yeah, he was scared.

Hicks said, "Okay. Tell Victor I'll meet with him tonight at eleven o'clock. Someplace in the open."

When Hicks spoke like that, quiet and calm-like, it made Dreamer think of the old Thomas. The young gangster that was strong and quick. Hard and violent. The man was driving a white truck now delivering white linen, wearing a windbreaker with the name of a company on it. Funny man, Thomas. Like he was playing at something or hiding. Still, his voice was cool . . .

Dreamer said, "I tell him." And got out at the next stop.

After the next delivery, Hicks drove to a Total gas station and made a call from the telephone booth.

The man answered the phone on the other end.

"Justin, yeah it's Thomas. Yeah, been a long time, brother. . . . I need to see you today. Yeah, that'll work."

Justin met him later and sold him a .40 caliber Ruger revolver for $450.00. Friend prices, Justin said. For old times' sake. Hicks wanted to smile then, but couldn't quite do it.

Cars and trucks rumbled over the expressways above, crossing over each other, held up by massive pillars. The pillars formed something like a small wood among the uncut grass, looking greener in the dark than in the daytime.

There was a dark blue van parked out there. Windows in the back, but you can't see through them because they've been darkened too. No other vehicles. In the distance a man walking alone. His form becoming human, taking shape as he gets closer to the van. Hicks.

When he got within twenty yards of the van, a large, heavyset man came out from the side of the van. Big shoulders and stomach. Then another man came out from the other side, big too, but not fat like the other one. Tree big, like a pro basketball player.

It was the second one that spoke first.

He said, "You Hicks?"

"Yeah."

"Why don't you take your hands out your pockets. We friends here."

"No we're not," Hicks said. "Where's Victor?"

"He's not here. He sent us."

"What he send you for?"

The big man that wasn't fat didn't feel like being coy.

"You know why."

"Well," Hicks said, "I don't actually. I figure if it ain't a hit, it's gonna be a beatin'. Which is it?"

"It's a beatin'. You don't take it, it becomes a hit. Understand?"

Hicks maintained eye contact with the big man.

The man spoke again, "I asked you if you understand," his voice harder now.

"I heard you, Jasper."

"Whoa. You a tough nigger. What you gonna do, shoot us all?"

"That's up to you."

"No, man. It's up to you. Victor being nice to you and you don't see it. You take a beatin' and you get to live. All you got to do is be a man and get it done."

"I can't do that."

"Boy, you gonna do it."

The big man moved toward Hicks.

Hicks said, "Stop."

But the man kept coming.

And in a split second, Hicks knew what would happen. He saw it all. The best that would happen is he would end up in the hospital with broken bones and contusions. Internal bleeding might kill him. And if it didn't, he'd lose his job because he'd be just another nigger that couldn't stay out of trouble after he clocked out, returning to his gang-bang life of fights and taking off work while he healed, the lazy bastard. Or they'd beat him to death. Or they'd beat him and then cap him and then he would be just as dead. He could not allow it. He could not allow any of it.

"Stop," Hicks said.

But the man he had called Jasper was closing in now, getting ready to do damage.

And Hicks shot him.

Pulled out the revolver and shot him in the chest. And then he heard Dreamer scream and he heard it as he saw it, heard the back doors of the van being kicked open as he saw a man there point a shotgun and Hicks stepped in front of the man he'd just shot, using him as a shield, then pushing him aside and letting him fall to the ground as he ran to his right and up and out of the shooter's range. And there was another blast, but it missed him. And the fat guy had a nine millimeter out and was popping it into the night, but then Hicks ran so that the van was between them and then Hicks kept running and when he got about twenty feet in front of the van, he slid to the ground. Waited.

It was quiet.

Then he heard shouts. *Where is he, he ran away, where'd he run to,* and so on.

Hicks waited.

And then he saw what he was waiting for. The man with the shotgun came to the front of the van to look out of the windshield. He looked for a count of about two when Hicks shot him through the glass. Once, then twice.

Hicks got up, scurried back toward the van, went to the left of it. He crouched down by the front tire.

"Jo-Jo! Jo-Jo! You hit? Jo-Jo."

Hicks saw the feet underneath the van, moving up to the driver's door. Hicks crept back, then around the van, then slowly turned the corner.

The fat guy was standing with the door open, looking at a dead man.

"Hey," Hicks said.

That got his attention. The fat man looked at him. He still had the 9 mm, but it was by his side, pointing toward the ground. Hicks had three shots left and the gun was pointed and ready.

Hicks said, "Let it drop, brother. You all alone now."

The fat man stared at him.

"I'm ready to die," he said.

"No, you ain't," Hicks said, giving him his prison stare. "Let it drop."

The fat man stared back for a moment, trying to save face. His chest heaved up and down, up and down. He let the gun slip from his fingers onto the grass.

Hicks said, "I ever see you again, I'll kill you. Now walk away."

The man walked, kept walking.

# TWO

The prairie north of Union City, Kansas is not flat but is rather a series of easy slopes. Wait till sunset, then pan slowly from right to left under the strong light of the western skies and it almost looks like the swell of the ocean after an April storm. Squint your eyes and listen to the sound of the wind pushing itself against the terrain. Try not to smell the grazing lands, not to smell the earth and you could be at sea. Isolated and alone and small. It is a harsh beauty.

A dirt road leaves the road and leads up through a field to a small, shabby house, the dirt road a brown stripe through yellow fields. The house on this prairie looks like it could be knocked down by a strong wind. The house does not enjoy the protection of cedar trees like many homes in this part of the country. The trees were never planted.

Outside the house is a green Plymouth Satellite. It is an old car, built in 1971 with the expectation of expiring around seven years later so that the owner will buy a new one. Or to be burned out on the stock car circuit within a couple of seasons. But it has survived over thirty years. Jett is a good mechanic. Though far too young to be its original owner.

There is a small barn in the back with two more vehicles in it. A VW bug and an International Jeep. Neither of them runs. The barn also has farming equipment in it. The equipment hasn't been used in fifteen years. At the back of the barn, there is a door that opens into an area that was used as

17

a stable. There is a methamphetamine kitchen there now.

At sunrise, Jett Penley stood on the front porch of the house eating a peanut butter sandwich. He washed it down with a glass of water because they were out of milk. The porch was built on the western side of the house and it gave him no view of the sunrise in the east. But he didn't care. He had spent most of his life in Kansas and the sunsets and sunrises and golden landscapes meant little to him. On that morning he was one week shy of his twenty-seventh birthday. A small, wiry man. He had tattoos on his shoulders and he shaved his head every three weeks. He didn't have any problems with blacks or Jews; he just shaved his head because that's how he liked it. It grew back fast.

Jett finished the sandwich and went inside the house and into the bedroom. Donna was still asleep in the bed. On her stomach, one leg crooked up, the other one straight. Her skin was pale with patches of color, some blue; she bruised easily. But she still looked good to Jett. Though better at night. Things were usually better at night.

Jett sat on the bed, scooted so that he was sitting up next to her. He lit a cigarette and stared at the wall for a while. Then he smacked the girl on her hip.

"Hey," he said. "Hey, sleepy. You need to get up."

Donna said, "mmmmhhh."

"Come on," Jett said. "We need to go."

"Where?" she said, her head still turned away from him.

"Kenny's," he said. "Come on, we need to get some milk too." He pinched her. "Come on."

She got out of bed, walked to the bathroom in her underwear and her tank top that said "Daddy's Little Girl" on it. After a while, Jett heard her brushing her teeth. Then heard her spit it out and wash it down the sink, then the water cut off.

Donna said, "Has Kenny got any money?"

"No."

She sighed out a *"ffffuck."* Like, you got me out of bed for this? "What are we doing then?"

"He's got a car," Jett said. "A Chevy truck. He wants to give us that."

"Jett, we got three cars already."

"It's a nice truck."

"He ain't gonna give you that truck unless you give him more crank. You know that."

Jett shrugged. He knew.

"Let's go," he said.

Jett and Donna got in the Satellite and shut the doors. The quiet morning sounds of nature were broken by the distinct sound of a Mopar engine coming to life. Jett put the car in gear and began a slow descent down the dirt road. He turned south on the paved road then accelerated. The car's automatic transmission shifted to a higher gear and drifted away.

It came out onto state road UU and made a right turn, headed west.

Behind it, a brown Ford Crown Victoria sat parked on the shoulder of the road. The driver started it and moved the column shift to drive. A police car. "Slick back," meaning there were lights and sirens in it, but not on top of it. If you looked through the back window, you could see two men in the front seat. They were brothers. The Wood Brothers. Behind the wheel was Garrett Wood. His neck was visible between the collar of his tan uniform shirt and the brim of his brown hat. Sometimes he didn't wear the hat, sometimes he did.

Next to him, Carl Wood. Carl did not wear a uniform.

He was not a police officer and he was not certified by the state to be in law enforcement. But Chief Bender had given him a commission as a Union City reserve officer. Carl Wood had a badge, but no uniform. His hair was longer than his brother's. Shaggy and wild, pushed back behind his ears. He wore jeans, boots, and a black T-shirt. He looked like a biker; rangy long arms and sunken cheeks. A monkey man. He no longer owned a bike though. He'd wrecked it in Logan County about a year earlier after going around a curve too fast. People were surprised—and disappointed—that he had not been killed. Disappointed mostly. Carl Wood said he didn't die easily.

Carl had grown up in Union City like his brother, but had left for a while. Spent a couple of years in Topeka working "security" jobs. Bouncing drunks at bars, keeping kids off the stage at concerts, and so forth. One time at a club, a college football player got mouthy with him, so Carl and another guy took him out to the alley and beat him almost to death. Carl was arrested and charged with assault and battery, but pleaded out to a two-year suspended sentence. With the understanding that his brother Garrett was to help him get back on the right path.

Carl and Garrett Wood. Years earlier, a woman said they should have been called Dead and Drift because neither one of them was worth a damn.

Garrett accelerated the car, caught up to the Satellite within a mile. Hit the flashers sitting on top of the dashboard.

The Satellite slowed, then pulled over to the side of the road. The police car came to a rest behind. Garrett turned to his brother.

"Stay here," he said.

Garrett walked up to the driver's side of the Satellite, his arms hanging at his sides. He didn't seem apprehensive or hurried. The window was rolled down when he got there.

Jett remained behind the wheel. He looked up at Assistant Chief Wood then back at his speedometer. He sounded bored when he spoke.

"H'lo Garrett."

"Jett."

Jett said, "Was I speeding?"

"A little bit," Garrett said. He looked through the window at Donna on the passenger side. She did not look back. Garrett said, "Where are you two headed this lovely morning?"

"Get some milk," Jett said.

"Get some milk." Garrett looked back at the Ford. Carl was staring back through the windshield. "Milk for your baby, huh." Looking at Donna again.

Looking at his rearview mirror, Jett said, "See you got your little brother with you, huh. Ride along day?"

"Carl?" Garrett said. "Just came along to keep me company."

Something was dawning on Jett then. Nothing he could fully explain at that moment, but a distinct feeling of dread. Jett looked back at the policeman.

"What do you want, Garrett?" Looking right at the man as he spoke, his voice mustering an even tone now.

It threw Garrett Wood off; courage from this crankster. Like someone had gotten to the punchline before him.

"Why so paranoid, Jett? You got something to hide?"

Jett said, "You want to arrest me, do it."

"Awww, now—"

"But if you're busting people for running drugs, you may want to start with the fellah in the car behind mine. He's a much bigger fish than me."

Garrett looked at Jett for a moment, looked at him as if

he were something distant or like he was an object. A deer or a bird. In his sights.

"You got that right," Garrett said.

Garrett Wood stepped back, pulling a .357 chief's special as he did so, and shot Jett Penley in the head. It knocked chunks out the other side, hitting Donna. She screamed and screamed and before Garrett got his bearings she had opened the door and was running away.

Garrett shot twice as she put distance between her and the car, but it was a short barreled revolver and was not accurate beyond a few yards. Carl stepped out of the Ford with a .223 rifle. He waited a moment before taking his shot, timing it. When he did Donna was trying to scramble up the bluff off the side of the road and Carl shot her in the back. Then shot her again after she fell.

Garrett said, "Make sure she's dead."

"She's dead," Carl said.

Garrett sounded like an impatient brother when he spoke. "Make sure, will you?"

# PART 2
## THURSDAY

# THREE

The phone rang and Maitland let Julie answer it. She was closer and they were in bed. The radio alarm had gone off twice putting NPR into their morning time for a few moments before Julie cut them off with the snooze. Nine more minutes of sleep, then nine more. Then the telephone.

"Hello," Julie said.

Maitland liked her voice in the morning. Throaty and unaffected. A woman's voice.

"Yeah, he's here."

She handed the phone to him, rolled away so her back was to him. "It's Mead," she said.

Looking up at the ceiling Maitland said yeah into the phone.

"Evan, it's Mead. You up?"

Charlie Mead of Mead's Bail and Bonds.

"Yeah," Maitland said.

"Sorry if I woke you."

Maitland peered over at Julie's backside, then at the clock. Seven thirty eight in the A.M. He was not a man of the morning. Thursday, he thought. It's Thursday.

"You didn't," Maitland said. "What's up?"

"I got a skipper. A big one."

"Yeah? How much?"

"Bonded out at two fifty. That's twenty-five thousand dollars if you bring him back."

Nothing if you don't, Maitland thought. But Mead didn't need to tell him that.

Maitland said, "Mmmm."

"He's dangerous, though, Evan. Shot and killed two men."

"And he's out on bond?"

"I'll explain that later. The guys he shot were jackboys for Victor Nelson. You know him?"

Maitland used to be a narcotics officer for the Chicago PD, but it had been years ago and the business changed hands so often.

"No, I don't know him. A gangster?"

"Yeah. He's a bad one. The skipper must have figured out he wasn't going to live too long whether or not he was convicted."

"What's his name?"

"Thomas Hicks. Black male, thirty years of age. Tall and strong and apparently pretty handy with a gun. Or lucky. You still interested?"

"Well, I like 'em tall."

"What?"

"Just kidding." Maitland looked at the swath of skin between Julie's panties and the bottom of her T-shirt. Two dimples equidistant from her spine. A stirring sight on a winter's morning or any other time for that matter. "You have any idea where he's hiding?"

"If I did, would I offer you twenty-five grand?"

Maitland said, "You mind coming by the store?"

"What's the hold up?"

"Well, I have to get permission from the wife."

"Which one?" Mead said.

"Fuck you." Maitland hung up.

He reached over Julie and hung the phone up, then put his hand on her hip. She was pretty. Fair skin, dark curly hair. She was a detective sergeant with the Chicago PD.

26

She had saved his life. Maitland let his hand rest on her hip.

Julie said, "What do you want?"

"Nothing."

Julie sighed. "There isn't time." She turned and looked up at him. "Maybe tonight."

It pissed him off. Maybe tonight. If you behave yourself and clean up your room. And, of course, let me come back here to stay the night. But it gave him something to look forward to and he knew it, and he knew that she knew it. Leveraging him into further commitment. Shit. Was it Pat Benatar that sang stop using sex as a weapon, stop using sex? Ah, well.

"Yeah, if I'm up to it."

"Right," she said, smiled and then kissed him. She stretched out of bed and walked toward the bathroom and Maitland watched her walk. Then got out of bed himself.

Evan Maitland and Julie Ciskowski were not married and they did not live together. That much he understood. Maitland lived alone in a two-bedroom walkup apartment on the north side. A brownstone apartment building with a pleasant garden in front. It was a nice place with wood floors and tasteful, modest furnishings. On the walls, there was a Manet sea print and Cezanne's still life apples along with a couple of oil paintings he had bought in the course of his antique business; all paintings of *things*, Julie said. No people. You like things better than people? And Maitland chuckled a non-response.

Maitland had married another woman at the age of twenty-eight, figuring it was time, divorced six years later realizing it wasn't. After the divorce, he turned the second bedroom of his into an office where he set up his computer on a table that he had bought for almost nothing because it was supposed to be a Chippendale but wasn't. He always thought he would marry again. Move out of the apartment and buy a house in the suburbs and start a family. And maybe he would. He was thirty-nine now and there was still time. But he had not discussed it with Julie Ciskowski. He told himself it was because she had only been divorced for a few months herself and she needed time to figure out where she was at and what she wanted, though he never asked her those questions directly.

He kissed her goodbye at the bottom of the fire escape, smelling her freshly shampooed hair as he did so. *Her* shampoo, he realized. Because, well, she had brought it over and left it in his bathroom. Okay then.

She got in the police department's take home Crown Victoria and drove away. Maitland backed his own car—a red '91 Mercedes Benz 560SEC two-door—out of the garage. He had bought the car a few months ago after totaling his BMW on the interstate. He missed the twelve-cylindered Bimm, but the 560 had a big engine too, the largest one Mercedes made at that time. Built to travel a smooth 140 on the autobahn or 90 on I-55 if you don't get popped, built at a time when a Mercedes wasn't built to look like a Lexus. After backing the car out of the garage, Maitland got out and shut the horizontal doors and locked them. It would be easier to have an automatic garage door that went up and down at the press of a switch, but the swinging doors were old wood ones that looked good and were, for him, worth the effort. Maitland liked old things.

He had gone into the antique business after leaving the police department. An antique dealer or a furniture salesman, depending on your point of view. He didn't mind being a salesman. And he knew antiques. He could tell a Louis XV table from French barn walls hammered together. He knew how to use the tools of his trade: magnifying glass, measuring tape, and magnet. He did not get emotionally attached to any wares and never exceeded his preset personal maximum bid at an auction. He dressed the part of the antique dealer: sportcoats, wool slacks, oxford shirts, cashmere sweaters. It was a uniform he did not mind wearing. When people found out that he used to be a police officer, they were usually surprised and would say ill-advised comments like, "I can see why that didn't last," as if only rockheads that had played high school football would choose to be a cop, not understanding that he had liked it for the most part and sometimes even missed it. But there was no point in getting upset with people or correcting them. People thought what they thought and usually you wasted time trying to explain things they wouldn't understand. They saw the clothes and the car and the furniture, but they didn't see the man. Generally, this was okay with Maitland.

He was co-owner of Casonne's Antiques, specializing in seventeenth and eighteenth century French and Italian collectibles like the sign said.

Maitland parked his car next to his partner's Range Rover.

His partner was a woman named Bianca Garibaldi. A stylish, attractive lady of forty. She had come to Chicago from Milan, Italy, twenty years earlier and married another man a few years after that. Maitland knew her husband and liked him. Bianca, the European, did not discuss the state of her marriage with Maitland. Or, Maitland suspected, with her husband either.

This morning she wore a dark sweater and black silk pants, a white shirt underneath, the lapels sticking out, and a sash around her waist. She knew how to dress. He could smell her perfume. Givenchy.

They had an office in the back of the store that they shared. Two desks facing each other, though they were rarely in there at the same time. Expensive rugs on the wood floors.

Bianca raised her eyes from paperwork on the table and said good morning and Maitland said good morning back.

Bianca pointed at a guitar in the corner behind Maitland's desk.

She said, "You buy that?"

"Yep."

"To serenade the girls?"

"No, ma'am. That is a Martin, made in 1942."

"We sell French and Italian antiques, not guitars."

"Well, we're selling that one. I picked it up in Pennsylvania last week for eighteen hundred dollars."

"Yes?"

"It's worth about twenty thousand."

"Really?"

A lock of hair draped over Bianca's eye and Maitland found himself looking at it.

"Yeah," he said.

"There's an auction in Maine in two weeks. Can you go?"

"I imagine I can."

"If you can't, I'll go."

"No, I'll go."

Bangor, Maine was a good auction. You could get good pieces if you knew what you were looking for and there weren't too many dealers there to drive up the bids. Bring them back clean and undamaged and sell them for a good profit. Be honest and smart, show a little class and gently remind the clientele that a good antique will outlast a great car.

Bianca said, "You sure you don't mind?"

"I don't mind."

"I know it's winter, but it's not too bad a place. Maybe you could take Julie with you. Keep you company."

"Yeah, maybe."

Maitland was not trying to reveal anything there, show a lack of enthusiasm or anxiety. It wasn't really Bianca's business anyway. But Bianca Garibaldi was a perceptive woman. Sometimes, it was a good thing. And sometimes it was a pain in the ass. She was Italian and she tended to say what was on her mind.

"Maybe not, huh?" she said. Almost smiling when she said it.

"Oh, shut up," Maitland said, smiling. "Listen, I've got Clara Brandt coming in today at ten. She wants to look at the armoire. Could you take care of her for me?"

"Sure. You have an appointment?"

Maitland hesitated. She's not your wife, he thought. But looking at him now like she was. It wasn't right. But she went back to her paperwork.

Maitland said, "Mead's coming by."

There was just a slight pause in her movement then. Looking at an invoice but not reading it. She started to read it again, then stopped.

"Mead," she said. Like she was affirming it.

Maitland looked directly at her. He would not apologize for it. She could eye him all she liked but he wasn't going to skulk around like a husband wanting permission to play golf.

"Yeah, Mead. The bail bondsman."

"I know who he is," she said, her voice a little tighter now.

"What?" he said. "Are you mad now?"

31

"You're a grown man, Evan. You do what you want to do."

"That's right," he said, thinking that would end it.

But it didn't. She said it again.

"You do what you want."

"So now you're going to pout?"

She held up her angry index finger.

"Don't patronize me. I do not like that."

"I know," Maitland said. "You've told me before."

She looked at him sharply for a moment and he looked back, holding in a smirk. And then she smiled and almost laughed. Then she shook her head.

She said, "You get shot again, I'm not coming to get you. Not again."

"I'm not going to get shot again. It's good money, Bianca."

"Oh, don't tell me that shit. You'll make as much money selling that guitar as you will chasing a criminal that skipped town. You're gonna be forty years old next year, Evan. How long you want to play this game?"

"It's not a game."

"It's a game," she said and walked out of the office, last wording him. Maitland looked at her bottom as she did so. Caught himself and shook his head.

Maitland said, "Bonded out on a murder charge?"

Charlie Mead said, "Impressive, huh? His lawyer is Sam Stillman. You know him?"

Maitland shook his head.

"Little guy, looks like a bantam rooster. You don't know . . . ? Anyway, he's a hotshot. Used to be a deputy district attorney, their star player. Resigned, ran for judge. Lost. So then he went into private practice and made a ton of money. Well, he's pretty well connected at county. He knew the judge. Pleaded self-defense for Hicks and got the judge to set bond at two fifty. Hicks got out of jail and bolted." Mead said, "Stillman is furious."

"Stillman refer Hicks to you or was it the other way around?"

"He referred Hicks to me."

"Then you're the one that should be mad."

"Damn right. Sam Stillman wanted a trial."

"Why?"

"He thinks he has a good chance of getting an acquittal. He says Hicks is innocent."

"Shit."

"No, he believes it. That's why he's so angry. He *believes* Hicks acted in self-defense. But by running away he's weakened that defense."

"What does Stillman think now?"

"Well . . . he still believes it was self defense."

"And he used to be a prosecutor?"

"Yeah."

"Has Hicks called Stillman since he fled?"

"No."

Maitland said, "I guess Hicks wasn't as optimistic."

"And you?" Mead said.

Maitland made a gesture to the man he considered his friend. He didn't have many friends.

Maitland said, "He killed two men and he didn't want to go back to jail. I don't know if he acted in self defense or not. Or care. I've been shot before and I don't want to go through that again."

Mead said, "It's a sizable bond. That's why I'm giving you the right of first refusal. But I think you should pass. I don't believe the guy acted in self-defense. Sam's persuaded himself that the guy did because that's what a good lawyer does. But you . . . you should stay here."

"If you think that, why did you call me?"

Mead said, "We're friends, aren't we?"

Yeah, they were friends. Partly because Mead understood him. Mead understood what Bianca probably did not and what Julie had not been in his life long enough to understand. It was not that he was sick or depraved or even particularly violent. It was that he needed to hunt. Finding hidden treasures in Maine didn't get it done. Bianca would be right if she said that there was more money to be made finding an Elizabethan chair and selling it. Profitable to be sure. But what was that? He needed to find men that did not want to be found and bring them back. A little screwed up, to be sure.

But he wasn't crazy.

Looking at the Martin guitar, Maitland said, "I can't do it for ten percent."

Mead said, "What are you asking for?"

"Twenty percent."

"That's fifty thousand dollars, Evan."

"That's right."

Mead smiled. He said, "I know five guys that'll do it for ten percent."

"Really," Maitland said. "For a violent shooter? And who, pray tell, are these guys?"

"Well . . ."

"Besides, I had hoped to make thirty thousand on the last job you sent me. And I didn't." Maitland left it out there.

Maitland was referring to the job in Oklahoma City. He found that skipper, but then he got shot and the skipper was taken away from him and killed. So Maitland didn't get paid.

Mead said, "That wasn't my fault."

"No one said it was," Maitland said. "It's the risk of the job, as we both know. But no one says I have to be stupid twice."

After a moment, Mead said, "No, no one is saying that. Okay. Fifty thousand."

# FOUR

It was easy enough finding the restaurant the lawyer owned. There was a big green sign above it that said "Sam's" and if that wasn't enough, there was a white Corvette parked in front with a tag that read "DEFENDER". Would that skippers would leave such marks.

Maitland parked behind the Corvette and went inside.

It was still morning so there weren't any customers. A bartender with a white shirt and a clean black apron asked Maitland if he could help him, his tone implying that he was in the wrong place. Maitland didn't take it personally, told the guy, no, he was here to see Mr. Stillman and the man was expecting him. The bartender nodded and left and then came back behind Stillman.

Sam Stillman did sort of look like a rooster. A small man with a large head, but tough looking. A distinct face, like an actor's. Not handsome, but expressive and memorable.

He said, "You the bounty hunter?" He seemed surprised.

"Yes."

"Oh," Stillman said. He extended a hand. "Sam Stillman. Can we sit?"

"Sure."

They went to a table in the main dining room.

Stillman said, "How long you known Charlie?"

"A few years."

"Charlie tells me you used to be a police officer."

"That's right."

36

"You know, I was with the D.A.'s Office?"

"I know."

"Did we ever meet before? On a case or something?"

"No."

The lawyer seemed to study him for a moment. Skeptical. Maitland thought about telling the man he had no reason to lie about it, but didn't.

Sam Stillman said, "Well, it was a big department." He gestured to the dining room and bar. "Ever been here before?"

It was a nice place. High ceilings, quality woodwork, oak bar. It must have cost him a fortune. Maitland knew lawyers that had made it and lawyers that had not made it. This one had made it. "No," Maitland said, "I haven't."

The lawyer seemed to have trouble believing it himself. He said, "It's crazy, isn't it? I grew up with nothing. Nothing. Went to school, got a job in the District Attorney's Office. I was going to stay there until retirement, but then Harris got elected D.A. and I was out. Then, with the belief that all my years of public service would count for something, I ran for judge and got about 35% of the vote. So at the lowest point of my life, I hang a shingle. And in the last three years, I've made more money than I did all the years before. I still can't believe it."

Maitland said, "It's a nice place." He didn't know what else to say.

"Well, you didn't come here to hear me talk about that." Stillman said, "You want to find Thomas?"

"Right."

"Okay. Attorney-client privilege aside, I have not heard from him in a few days."

"Did he tell you he was going to leave?"

"I wouldn't tell you if he did. But, no. He did not."

"Did he give you any indication that he would?"

"No. I'm not sure he trusts me."

"He hired you."

"That doesn't mean anything. Don't get me wrong, it doesn't hurt my feelings. Most clients don't trust me at first. But then we get in the heat and they come around."

"Does he owe you money?"

"No."

"Do you care if he comes back?"

"As a matter of fact, I do. I expended a lot of political capital getting him bonded out. And now he's left town and put me in a bind."

"That's unfortunate."

"Yes, it is. Yes it is unfortunate. I want him back here for trial."

Maitland remembered what Charlie had told him. *Why would an innocent man run?* Put that question to a jury and he's halfway convicted right there. Maitland said, "Why? I mean, why don't you just forget about it? People jump bail all the time. It's not a reflection on you."

"That's where you're wrong. It is a reflection on me. When I give my word to a judge that I've known for fifteen years that this guy's going to show up for trial and he leaves town, I've lost that ability for any other person that wants to hire me. I've lost more than that, really. You understand that, don't you?"

"Yeah, I understand."

"Besides," Stillman said. "I think he's innocent."

Maitland smiled, though he tried not to. The guy seemed all right for a lawyer.

"Seriously," Stillman said. "I do. I'll tell you something right now: you bring him back here and I'm going to get him acquitted. You do that and you can eat here anytime you like. On the house." The lawyer was smiling now; performing and enjoying it. He said, "I mean it. No one knows better than me how to do it. I'll show those guys how this shit works."

Maitland thought, *those guys?* God, it's a game to him. Well . . . so what if it was.

Maitland said, "But hasn't Hicks screwed the case already? He ran. They're going to say to the jury, innocent men don't run."

"Sure they do," Stillman said. "Besides, I'm not worried about that. I'll keep it out; the jury will never hear about it."

A confident man, Maitland thought. A very confident man. "Well," Maitland said, "good luck with all that. But we need him here first."

Stillman heard what he was saying. He said, "Look, if I had any idea where he was, I'd tell you. I'd go with you, in fact. But I don't know where he is."

"Yeah?"

"Yeah. To you, he's worth money. Ten percent of the bond. Okay, fair enough. To me, he's worth more than that."

Yeah, Maitland thought. An opportunity to show the District Attorney's Office how this shit works. Maitland wondered then if you needed to have money, a lot of money, to understand the lack of happiness it could bring. The man had the car and house and his own restaurant. But it wasn't satisfying him. No, what he really wanted to do was pull the pants off some guys at the District Attorney's Office. Maybe give a few juicy quotes to a television reporter after the trial. And just about everyone would forget about it within a week, but the victors and the losers would not forget.

"Besides," Stillman said, "I kind of like the guy."

Maitland thought this was strange, coming from a man that had been a prosecutor. Their views of human nature were generally as cynical as the cops'. The criminally accused were called turds, losers, douche bags, gangbangers, fuckers, or motherfuckers. They weren't called Thomas.

Maitland said, "I suppose that helps."

"It helps," Stillman said, "but it's not necessary."

Maitland paused.

Then said, "How do you know he's not dead?"

"Dead?"

"My understanding is, he shot a couple of guys sent by a kingpin. A guy named—?"

"Victor Nelson."

"Yeah, Victor Nelson. How do you know he hasn't had Hicks killed?"

Stillman said, "I guess I don't. But Thomas is not so easy to kill."

Stillman would not give him a complete copy of his file, but he did give Maitland all the police reports he had, as well as any material he had received from the District Attorney's Office. Maitland took the copies Stillman's office provided and looked over them during lunch at a delicatessen on State Street. The arrest report, witness statements, the counts filed by the prosecutor. There were a couple of fuck you letters between Stillman and one of the assistant D.A.'s that were interesting but didn't help explain where Thomas Hicks was and whether or not he was alive.

The reporting officer had written that at approximately 2115 hours he, Patrolman Nick Scapek, Badge #3822, of the Chicago Police Department heard via Police Band Radio, Precinct 23 Police Dispatch advising all available units to converge underneath the viaduct near the intersection of Eighty-Seventh and Chatham Road. Immediately following the broadcast he heard Corporal Jones on the radio advising that shots were fired. Officer Scapek activated the Red/Blue Emergency Lights and Audible Siren and drove to the scene. Upon arrival at the scene, he removed his riot gun from his patrol car. He then observed a black male in his late twenties/early thirties walking toward a light blue 1978 Chevrolet Monte Carlo. Officer Scapek identified himself as a police officer, drew his service weapon and requested that the suspect place his hands on the hood of the Chevrolet Monte Carlo. Suspect complied. Officer Scapek searched said suspect and removed a .40 caliber Ruger revolver. Corporal Jones, Badge #2976, then arrived and assisted Officer Scapek in arresting said suspect.

Maitland remembered his days as a young patrolman. His reports had probably not sounded much different from Officer Scapek's. Earnest, scared . . . it was a rush, capturing a suspect and not getting shot in the process.

Maitland read the rest of the material, including the record of Hicks' prior arrests and convictions. The man Sam Stillman called Thomas had been a gangbanger and had done hard time. He'd stayed out of trouble for a few years after he got out, but the old habits came back.

Not that the guys he killed were angels. Maitland smiled, thinking about how the prosecutors would try to portray the victims. Good young men with bright futures. Maitland knew how that game was played.

He leaned back in his chair. A waitress asked him if he wanted more coffee and he said, thanks, he would. He could hear city noise outside: cabs, buses, horns and it comforted him.

He wondered about Thomas Hicks surrendering peacefully to the police, even though he had the gun on him.

Was Hicks alive?

His lawyer seemed to think so. Why though? What did the lawyer know? Had the lawyer kept something from him? *I know, but I'm not telling you.* Why play that game?

Maybe the lawyer didn't know. He just believed Hicks was alive. Believed in his client, so he wanted him to be alive.

Maitland thought about gangster grudges. Usually, they were over stupid, petty things. But more often than not, they were short term. Something worth killing for on Saturday could be forgotten by Wednesday.

So which was this? If it were a long-term grudge, odds were Hicks was dead and time and money spent looking for him would be wasted. But wait. Not necessarily. If they wanted to kill him, it might explain him skipping bond. He would need to hide just to stay alive.

Still, if the man was dead, Maitland would need to know.

Maitland signaled the waitress for the check.

Maitland met Jeffrey "don't call me Jeff" Gasa three years earlier when a neighbor of Jeffrey's had skipped bond on a drug distribution charge. Jeffrey was a short, stocky black man in his early fifties. He called Maitland and told him who he was and said, "I understand you looking for Goldy."

Maitland said he was.

Jeffrey said, "Yeah, that's what I thought you said. His mother's a friend of mine. I'm calling for her, you understand."

"Okay," Maitland said.

"See, Goldy's a dumbass kid. You try to take him in, he liable to try something stupid and you'll probably have to shoot him. See, I don't want that to happen."

Maitland said he did not want that to happen either.

Jeffrey said, "What I'm saying is, I want to work with

you. Get him to come with you peaceably."

Maitland wondered why he would want to do that.

Jeffrey said, "He's stupid, but I don't want him hurt, see. His mother's good people."

Maitland was wary, but he agreed to at least talk with Jeffrey Gasa. They met outside his house.

There were a lot of old cars in the driveway; some in working order, some being worked on. There was a '66 Thunderbird for sale. Jeffrey caught Maitland looking at it and said, "She's pretty, ain't she? I can give it to you for $5500.00."

"No thanks," Maitland said.

Jeffrey Gasa told Maitland about himself. He was a bus mechanic for the city and he owned some rental property in the neighborhood. He rented one of his units to Goldy's mother. Though not Goldy. But it was Goldy's mother's place that Goldy was in. It didn't take long for Maitland to figure out that Jeffrey Gasa would be glad to see Goldy pulled out of the rental unit himself.

Jeffrey said, "Usually, I go into these situations, I got two things: a gun and my cellphone; speed dial set to 911."

Maitland said, "I understand that."

"This is a rough neighborhood," Jeffrey said. "Last year? I was walking right over there, middle of the day, and these two junkies jumped me. I clocked the shit out of one and he ran off. But the other one didn't get away and I did a Mexican tap dance on his ass."

Maitland regarded the man. About fifty, but he looked like he could do it.

Jeffrey looked into the rental unit from the sidewalk. "Well," he said, "let's get this done. Hey. You mind staying out here? I'm going to try to talk him into coming out here."

"Okay," Maitland said. "Will you be all right?"

"Don't worry about me."

Fifteen minutes later Jeffrey Gasa walked out with Goldy. Jeffrey raised his hand to Maitland, telling him it was cool. Goldy did not struggle as Maitland put handcuffs on him and took him away.

He put him in the car and came back to Jeffrey Gasa to thank him.

Jeffrey said, "That's all right. Thanks for working with me."

Jeffrey Gasa saw the confusion in Maitland's face and decided he would explain himself to the man. He said, "We have to live here, man." Meaning, we don't want any gunfire if we can avoid it. Maitland said, "Okay." He understood.

After that, Jeffrey would call him from time to time. Ask him to find people or refer him someone to refer to Charlie. Maitland called him a couple of times. He tried to help when he could.

Now, Maitland called him from the delicatessen and asked if he could come talk to him. Jeffrey said to come on over. Maitland got to the man's house.

Jeffrey said, "Come look at my new pool."

They walked to the back yard where he had had the pool installed. Jeffrey pointed to the wooden patio and the small shed that held the cleaning equipment and the crack in the cement that was pissing him off. Maitland told him he should hire a lawyer and look into going after the contractors.

"No," Jeffrey said. "I'll take care of it." And there was a look on his face that said he no doubt would.

Maitland suppressed a smile. Then he walked around the pool as Jeffrey took a call on his cellphone; he was often on the phone. The pool was empty and cold and white. He would rather talk in the house where it was warm, but Jeffrey had wanted him to see this. Maitland put his hands in his coat pockets.

Jeffrey walked over. "Sorry," he said. "What's up?"

"A guy named Thomas Hicks. He killed two men a few nights ago, got arrested and jumped bond. You know him?"

"Man, you think we all know each other?"

Maitland smiled.

"No, I don't think that."

"Okay," Jeffrey said, nodding . . . performing, but not smiling. "These boys worked for Victor Nelson, right?"

"Yeah, that's right."

"Well, I don't know Hicks. I know who Victor is, though."

Maitland said, "Yeah?"

"My understanding is, a dumbass feud over a lady. People always wanting to die over pussy."

"Hicks went after Victor's woman?"

"No. It was his little brother's woman. Maybe. His little brother's a punk. But Hicks smacked him around and Victor had to do something about it." Jeffrey said, "That's how it is with these pimps. Always havin' to make sure no one's disrespecting them."

Maitland waited for him to say something else. He didn't.

Maitland said, "So?"

"So he sent a couple of boys after Hicks and I guess he was ready."

Maitland said, "Is he alive now?"

"Who?"

"Hicks."

Jeffrey said, "I don't know."

Maitland would not push Jeffrey Gasa. He said, "Okay."

He started to go.

45

Jeffrey said, "Hold on." He lowered his voice. "The boy you want to talk to is Dreamer Rasheed."

"Who's that?"

"He's someone that would know if the man were dead or alive."

"How would he know?"

Jeffrey shook his head. There were limits to what he would say. Which was understandable. As he had said to Maitland before, he had to live here. Jeffrey said, "He would know. That's all I can tell you."

"Can you tell me where to find him?"

"Usually, you can find him at the Fairfax Hotel."

"Okay."

Jeffrey said, "You understand, I can't go with you there."

"I won't ask you to," Maitland said.

They shook hands and Maitland turned to go.

He heard Jeffrey Gasa behind him.

"Be careful, Evan."

Maitland kept walking, held up his arm and waved.

A city bus roared past the front of the Fairfax and Maitland crossed the street in its wake. He walked in the lobby of the Fairfax and found himself in a dark, poor place. A faint smell of urine and radiator heat. It was the sort of place Maitland's ex-wife used to ask how people could live in. She lived in the suburbs now, remarried with children.

There was a heavyset black man behind the counter; an older man. He looked briefly at Maitland, sensing his presence and the fact that he was alien to this place. Then bent back over his newspaper. Maitland believed the man thought he was a cop. And that was okay. He walked over to the counter.

Maitland said, "I'm looking for Dreamer Rasheed."

The man shrugged, barely. He kept his eyes on the newspaper on top of the counter.

Maitland put two twenties on top of the newspaper.

A moment passed. The guy did not look up, but after a moment his hand was on the counter and on top of the money. He said in a voice just above a whisper, "1012."

Maitland took the elevator to the tenth floor. When he got off the elevator, his heart rate quickened. He remembered a couple of drug raids he had gone on when he was a patrolman, usually in the background. The silence, eight to ten guys creeping down a hallway not much different from this one. The hand signals. Then the silence broken by the battering ram or, in some cases, a shotgun and then nothing but noise. Men shouting, drawing weapons. Scary then. Scarier if you were doing it alone.

Maitland reached the door and knocked. Knocked again. He heard a television. Then he didn't. Turned off or muted.

Then:

"Who is it?"

"A friend."

"What do you want?"

"I want to talk to Dreamer."

"He ain't here."

Maitland said, "You got Hicks in there?" He waited.

A man opened the door and said, "Who the fuck are you?"

A black guy in his face. Angry eyes. The guy was younger than Maitland, maybe in his early twenties. There were two other guys in the room, sitting on the couch behind a coffee table with tin foil and other fast food packaging on it, among other things. The man at the door stepped back; as if to say, come on in if you got the nuts. Maitland stepped in and heard the door shut behind him.

Having done that, he realized he had probably made a mistake. One of him and three of them. The guy that had opened the door was standing off to Maitland's right now and the two guys sat on the couch in front of him, one of them looking pretty hard-on himself. But it was the junkie looking one that did not seem angry that Maitland kept an eye on.

He looked at that one and said, "You Dreamer?"

"Yeah, man. What you want?"

"I'm looking for Thomas Hicks."

"He ain't here."

"Do you know where he is?"

The one standing to his right said, "You a cop?"

"Yeah," Maitland said.

"Where's your badge?"

"I left it in the car."

The one standing was the one doing the talking, saying "shit" now because he didn't believe him. Fair enough. But it was the guy sitting next to Dreamer on the couch that concerned him. It was always the quiet ones you had to worry about; they did not talk shit or try to show you how big their units were; they thought about moving and then they moved.

Maitland said to the quiet guy on the couch, "How about you? You know where Hicks is?"

The man on the couch looked right back at him, but did not say anything.

And Maitland thought, yeah, this could get bad.

Maitland looked at Dreamer. He said, "Is Hicks alive?"

"Man, I don't know what you're talking about."

Dreamer got off the couch and started to move into the kitchen.

Maitland knew it was coming then. The quiet man on the couch moved his shoulders forward; it was slight, but it meant that he was starting to get up and it was not something you could wait for, you had to move first because these guys were faster and younger and they were going to move on him. So Maitland kicked at the coffee table and then pushed it up and over on top of the man on the couch, upsetting the soda cups and everything else on the table as he pushed it back against the man, leaning on it with most of his weight as he took his .38 out of his coat pocket and put it on the man to his right.

"Back off," Maitland said.

The man on his right stayed where he was, not backing away but not coming forward either, seeing something in Maitland's eyes that made him believe the man would pull that trigger and put a hole in his midsection. The man was not going to move back any further, wanting to save face because he was young and stupid and brave over the wrong things. So Maitland backed away so that he could see the kitchen, and fuckin'-A, Dreamer crawling out the kitchen window and climbing down the fire escape.

"Goddammit," Maitland said.

He went into the kitchen and went out the window onto the fire escape, keeping his eyes on the men inside until he was down a flight of stairs. Then he looked down to see Dreamer reach the last flight and the kid just jumped down onto the sidewalk without even using the sliding ladder. Something Maitland would not even attempt if he were fifteen years younger. Maitland reached the landing and pushed the ladder down its rails, climbed down.

Once on the sidewalk, he looked up to see if either of the guys in the apartment were coming after him. He saw that they were not, put his gun back in his coat pocket and started running after Dreamer.

Jesus, it sucked. Running in the cold, one lung pumping all the breath he had. He had quit smoking after he lost the lung and he had kept his weight down to keep as little strain on his respiratory system as possible, but it still hurt to run in the cold if you weren't used to doing it. What kept him going, apart from the hunter's instinct, was the notion that that man he was chasing was a junkie who had only a sugar burst of energy in him, but would not be able to run more than two or three blocks before tiring out. If he could just outlast the man.

He chased him for three city blocks and it still felt miserable, wondering if it was worth it, if he should try to start running regularly for exercise and if he did would he have to dress like the coffee shop joggers he casually disdained. And then watched as Dreamer jumped over a turnstile to the elevated train and started running up a stairway—shit, he was going for the train. If he got on board, he would be gone and Maitland would have a long angry walk back to his car.

But then Maitland got to the stairway and ran up the first flight and then halfway up the second flight breathed a sigh of relief as he saw Dreamer pushing against a gate that was locked. He had chosen the wrong stairway.

Maitland slowed as he approached Dreamer. He pulled the gun back out and showed it to the man. He told Dreamer to turn around and put his hands against the gate. Dreamed did so and Maitland patted him down for weapons. He didn't want to do all this work only to get stabbed or poked with a needle. He didn't find anything and he turned Dreamer around.

Dreamer said, "I just forgot, that's all."

Maitland said, "Forgot what?"

"My court date. I thought it was next week."

"Court date?" Maitland frowned. Oh. The guy had jumped bond himself. On who knows what. Maitland said, "You thought I was after you?"

"Aren't you?"

"No, god—" Maitland was suddenly angry. "No, I'm not after you. Didn't you hear what I said?"

Dreamer Rasheed stared back at him with milky eyes. Disconnected. "What?" he said. Fucking junkie.

"Thomas Hicks," Maitland said. "I only want to talk to you about Thomas Hicks."

Another pause while Dreamer tried to process it. "Yeah. Thomas a good boy."

Maitland rubbed his face. Fear and anger and the adrenalin rush had exhausted him. He said, "Are you thirsty?"

"Yeah. Kind of."

"Me too," Maitland said. "Come on, I'll buy you a Coke."

In the bodega, Maitland put a twelve-ounce can of Dr Pepper and bottled water on the counter. Dreamer said he liked Dr Pepper. Maitland watched, rolled his eyes, as Dreamer placed a couple of candy bars next to them. The cashier rang it all up and Maitland paid for it.

They stood outside, drinking beverages in the cold as traffic and people went by.

Maitland said, "How long have you known Thomas?"

"We grew up together," Dreamer said. "That long."

"You know he was arrested."

"That right? I didn't know nothing about that."

Maitland frowned. "You got a bench warrant out on you. I can make a phone call and have you taken in or I can not make that call. So help me out, all right?"

"Heyyyy. No need to talk like that. Yeah, I know he was arrested."

Maitland said, "They can't find him now."

"I know," Dreamer said. "They been lookin' too."

Maitland had meant the police. But he snagged on something Dreamer had said.

"They?" Maitland said. "You mean, Victor's people?"

"Yeah. I told them same as I told you. I don't know where the man is."

Maitland thought, here was something. Jeffrey Gasa knew what he was doing. Maitland said, "When did you tell them this?"

"When did I tell Victor's people?"

"Yeah."

"This morning. It's the truth, too. I do not know where the man is."

Maitland said, "Do you think he's alive?"

"Well, I 'magine he is. They ain't found him."

Well . . . shit. Hicks was alive and hiding somewhere. Good news, on the surface. It meant there was still a chance to make a $50,000.00 fee bringing Hicks in. Yes, Maitland thought, it should be good news. But the scene in Dreamer's place lingered with him. They could have closed on him and taken his gun away from him and killed him with it. Or they could have just thrown him off the fire escape. It was over now and they hadn't managed to do it and Maitland had not lost his nerve. . . . probably not lost his nerve. But it gave him a feeling of bad karma about the whole thing. A violent shooter with violent enemies. He could catch the guy, escort him peacefully to his car only to be cut down in a hail of bullets from guys sent by Victor Nelson. Cue the Warner Brothers cartoon music as Porky Pig says, *Thhhhattt's all ffffolks.*

He realized, with some shame, that part of him would have been relieved to learn that Thomas Hicks *had* been killed. Because then it would be over and there would be nothing else for him to do; go back to the antique shop and have Bianca shake her head at him some more and then slip back into the routine of selling furniture.

Maitland studied Dreamer for a moment.

Maitland said, "You know something of this thing between Hicks and Victor Nelson?"

Dreamer said, "Man, everybody know about it."

"Do you know more than everybody?"

Dreamer Rasheed was looking away from him.

Maitland said, "Were you there?"

Dreamer knew what he meant and Maitland knew he knew.

Dreamer said, "No."

"Hey, don't lie to me. I bought you a Coke."

Dreamer Rasheed said, "Man. What do you care? You with the bail bondsman; you're not his lawyer."

Yeah, Maitland thought. He was there. His name had not appeared in any of the police reports or lists of potential witnesses, but he was there. But he was right. It shouldn't make any difference to Maitland. Maybe it would to Hicks. But Hicks would know if he was there already. It was between Hicks and his lawyer. And this man. Maitland had a rule when it came to these things and that rule was: do not become a witness. *The suspect told me . . . the witness seemed to know who was there . . .* It was too much trouble.

Maitland said, "And you don't know where he is?"

"If I knew, don't you think I would have told them?"

After a moment, Maitland said, "Yeah, I guess you would."

Maitland walked away from the man, leaving him with the pop and candy bars.

Back in his car, Maitland realized that he would have to

talk to the police next. It was not something he looked forward to. He had left the Department under a cloud; amidst accusations of corruption and murdering a witness to his alleged graft. He knew he was clean and did not really care much who believed him or who did not. But some of them remembered him and thought he was dirty and treated him accordingly. His ego was big enough that he would get angry at comments or even jokes about being crooked. Sometimes he almost wished he had been on the take; at least then he would have profited from the shit he sometimes had to take. Add to that the fact that he was now sleeping with Julie Ciskowski. A Chicago PD detective who was very attractive and had risked her career to save him. After her divorce he had started seeing her and the glares and cold silences among police officers had not gone unnoticed by him. Cops are tribal and they believed, perhaps understandably, that once Julie Ciskowski got divorced, she should have ended up with one of them, not some disgraced ex-cop that sold furniture to rich people in Lake Forest. The problem was further complicated by the fact that, to a degree, Maitland envied them because they were commissioned police officers, some of them wearing the badge of detective. Which he had never managed to do. And never would. It was a stupid thing to feel regret over. He knew it led him to do stupid and unnecessary things, like asking Dreamer Rasheed if he was there when Hicks shot the two guys. It was not his place to ask such questions and even a junkie like Dreamer knew it.

The police weren't much help.

One of the problems was that the homicide had already been solved. The arrest had already been made and the District Attorney's Office had already filed their counts. Two black males of dubious background were dead and the police were not overwhelmed with grief. After Thomas Hicks had fled, police officers had searched his home and the homes of what little family he had in the area and that was pretty much that. There was not going to be what the news media called an "intensive manhunt." Though official "manhunts," in Maitland's experience, were rarely much use anyway.

When he was a patrol officer, a prisoner had escaped from a county jail near Rockford and killed an elderly couple who lived on a farm. Then he ran on foot because he couldn't find the keys to their car. There followed the "intensive manhunt." Local deputies, town police officers, and a few Chicago and Rockford cops combed the bleak countryside looking for the killer. They called it off after two and a half weeks because the overtime pay was skyrocketing and they weren't getting anywhere. The killer was apprehended two weeks after that in southern Illinois after he was shot by a retired doctor who kept a pistol hidden under the driver's seat of his Ford van. Turned out the killer had been hiding in north Illinois the entire time the police were searching for him. He only left after they called off the search and he carjacked the doctor and his wife.

It was not until driving three hundred miles south that the doctor saw his opportunity and took it, shooting the predator, saving his own life and his wife's. At a press conference afterwards the doctor said he was relieved that he had not killed the man. Maitland suspected he was not the only one with a different worldview.

The homicide detective who arrested Hicks turned out to be a tall, thin guy with a crew cut. He was a handsome and stoic man who wore a charcoal suit and a starched white shirt with a red tie, aware of his looks. He affected the elite carriage of homicide, like he was posing for a television cameraman that he hoped would show up. But he was helpful if you were willing to listen to him talk about himself for a while and nod your head to acknowledge his importance. His name was Alan Kimmel.

Standing in the parking lot of a hot dog stand, he told Maitland the case against Hicks had been solid. He said, "The witness saw him shoot the two guys."

Maitland said, "Who was the witness?"

Detective Kimmel said, "A guy named Marcus Gilman."

"What about him?"

"What do you mean, what about him?"

"I mean what was he doing there?"

The detective hesitated, looking at Maitland. "Why do you care?"

They were across the street from Wrigley Field. A cool day in mid-March. The skies were gray and they had to speak over the sounds of lunchtime traffic. Alan Kimmel leaned back against the unmarked police car, his tan overcoat pushed back, hands in his pants pockets. He was a policeman and policemen are quick to distrust.

Maitland said, "I'm not working for his lawyer, if that's what you're thinking. It helps if I know how the skipper thinks. You understand that."

After a moment, the detective said, yeah, as if he knew it all along, and Maitland had to suppress a smile.

Detective Kimmel said, "Well, between you and me, Marcus didn't really have much of a good reason to be there. He just said he was there with his friends. But as Stillman probably knows, Marcus is no cherry. Got about four, maybe five arrests. But we've got two dead men and all the evidence says Hicks killed them."

"Hicks has a record too," Maitland said. "But was he clean until this?"

"You mean between the time he got out of prison eight years ago . . . ?"

"Yeah."

"Yeah, I think he was, more or less. He had a job."

"Has he got family?"

Kimmel turned to look at his partner, who was now walking up to them, holding two hot dogs in a box. Maitland could smell the cucumber slices and mustard. The partner looked more like a cop: stocky and balding, about ten years older than Kimmel. He had introduced himself earlier as Frank Ferney.

Frank said, "What?"

Kimmel said, "He wanted to know if Hicks had a family."

"Oh," Frank said. "Well he doesn't have a father. His mother died years ago. He had a brother, Edward Hicks. He was shot and killed."

"Yeah?" Maitland said, "When was that?"

"Three, four years ago. Just a random thing. Standing on the wrong corner at the wrong time. He was clean. A civilian. Just on the wrong corner during a drive by. Or he happened to look like the wrong guy. It was heartbreaking."

"This thing with Thomas Hicks," Maitland said, "is it related to his brother?"

Frank said, "You mean like a payback? No. I know the guys that investigated it. It was a long time ago. Anyway, that was all the immediate family he had. We've checked other places in town. Cousins, and so forth. Nothing."

Maitland said, "Does he have a girl?"

Kimmel said, "Not that we could find."

"Kids?"

Frank said, "No. No kids."

Kimmel said, "It's a big city. A lot of places to hide, but he has to buy groceries, get out sometime. They all come out sometime. Or someone will turn him in."

Maitland said, almost to himself, "I think he left town."

Kimmel, feeling a bit challenged, said, "Why do you think that?"

"Well, wouldn't you?"

Kimmel said, "I wouldn't have done what he did." Missing the point of the question.

Frank said, "Maitland—that's your name?"

"Yeah."

"You used to be with Chicago PD, didn't you?"

"Yeah."

"Did you used to work narcotics?"

"Yeah. That was a long time ago."

The detective named Frank seemed to study him for a moment. He knows something about my past, Maitland thought. But Maitland wasn't going to help him. And he wasn't going to defend himself either. He just looked back at the detective to show him he was not ashamed of anything. Detective Kimmel looked at his partner for a moment, confused. He could see that something was passing between his partner and the bounty hunter, something he was not in on.

Frank decided to let the sleeping dog sleep. He said, "Well then you know that guys like Hicks usually don't ever leave their own neighborhoods. It's too much for them."

Maitland said, "That's true of most ghetto criminals. But Hicks may not have been like most. In fact, I'm not altogether sure he was. He was straight for eight years."

Frank said, "Maybe so. But he stayed in his neighborhood."

Maitland smiled. He didn't mind a little friendly competition. And part of him missed the give and take of cop talk. Still, he thought this detective was wrong. But he needed the man's help.

"Can I see his apartment?" Maitland said.

# FIVE

A one-room efficiency on the Southside, clean and minimally furnished. There were free weights on the ground. A small television, no cable, and a newspaper on the floor. On top of the television there was a videotape of the third Ali–Frazier bout. Maitland held it up for a moment, reading the back.

Frank the detective said, "That the one in Manila?"

Maitland said, "I think so."

"You ever see that fight? They went fourteen rounds and just beat the living shit out of each other. Held nothing, I mean nothing, back. You can't believe a man can take that and stay on his feet."

"Which man?" Maitland said.

"Both," Frank said. He went into the bathroom and shut the door behind him.

Detective Alan Kimmel was downstairs in the car. He had not openly opposed going this far to help Maitland, but he had made a point of brooding and shaking his head to show them he disapproved. His partner seemed not to notice.

Maitland looked for a sign, a bread crumb of where to go next. A piece of paper with a girl's telephone number on it, a set of written directions. Gimme clues, but it was surprising how dumb a lot of skippers could be. Maitland had once found a guy because he left a specific address on his girlfriend's answering machine. People act more out of habit and emotion than they do reason and this is particularly true of skippers. They run because they're frightened

59

and anxious. Most of them do not think about the long term. A good many of them know they'll eventually be caught, but if they can just be free one more day, maybe two . . . maybe the police and the bail bondsmen will forget about them and concentrate on someone else, maybe a witness will die, maybe they'll die, maybe they'd wake up and realize the whole thing had been a bad dream. Like any hunter, Maitland knew that they would run to food, shelter, and poontang. Girlfriends and mothers were usually glad to provide shelter.

But Thomas Hicks's mother was dead. And there was no sign that he had a girlfriend.

Maitland looked out the apartment window. All it offered was the view of another wall of another depressing apartment building. Did it seem bleak to Hicks when he looked out the same window? Jesus, he thought. Fifteen minutes in low income housing and he was thinking like a liberal.

He looked at the couch positioned in front of the television. For a moment, he contemplated sitting on it and trying to see if he could think like the skipper. If I were Hicks, where would I go? . . . ah, that would be a waste of time.

He went into the kitchen and opened the refrigerator. Milk, orange juice, an egg carton with eggs in it, and nothing else.

He opened drawers in the kitchen, found knives, forks, cooking utensils . . . a flash of color beneath. He closed the drawer and then something hit at him. He opened the drawer back up.

There was a newspaper clipping beneath the silverware.
Maitland pulled it out.

It was a clipping from *The Kansas City Star*.

The clipping was faded to yellow, but the newsprint was legible. Splashes of color in the photo next to the story. Young men, athletes, celebrating a victory on the basketball court. *Kansas State Upsets Georgia Tech.*

In smaller print beneath, it read: "Advances to Sweet Sixteen." Then in smaller print beneath that it said, "Hicks named MVP."

Detective Frank Ferney came out of the bathroom.

Maitland said, "Edward Hicks was a basketball player?"

"I don't know."

Maitland scanned the article. Edward Hicks had played well. Scored twenty-two points and three field goals. There was a look of joy and optimism and youth in his face that would be forever enshrined in the photo. Shit, it was a hard life.

Maitland read the entire article. Then re-read it. After that he was reasonably sure he had found Thomas Hicks.

# SIX

Maitland made the call from his apartment.

"Hello."

"Hey, it's me."

"Hey."

Julie's voice was warm and welcoming on a cold late afternoon, so from the start he felt bad.

"Listen," Maitland said, "I've got to leave town."

"Oh. What's up?"

"Ah, skipper. He's probably in Kansas." Maitland was quiet, waiting.

And Julie said, "You're still going to do that?"

"Well, I never told you I wouldn't." He tried to say it gently, but when he heard himself speak it sounded pretty lame and defensive. As if not volunteering information was the same thing as telling the truth. Hey, it depends on what the definition of the word *is* is. "Ah, shit, Julie," he said. "I just need to do this, okay? You should understand." He meant, since she was a police officer.

But he wasn't sure she did. Maybe she did and maybe she didn't. But if she did, he screwed it all up with the next thing he said.

She said, "Well, I'll see you back at the apartment when you get back."

And he said, "Yeah, I'll call you."

He knew it was a mistake right away. No, no, no. You were supposed to say, sure. Or, I look forward to that. Or, you'd be so nice to come home to, so nice by the fire. Not,

I'll call you. Because if you say that, then the woman knows you've got a fair amount of anxiety over the thought of living together, and it's going to cost you. You don't say it to a woman as perceptive and as tough as Julie Ciskowski.

Relax, he thought. Maybe she missed it.

"Well, don't knock yourself out," Julie said and hung up the phone.

Maybe not.

He put the phone down and contemplated the empty, quiet apartment for a moment. Then he got his stuff packed. Clothes, papers, handcuffs, weapons. A .38 snub revolver and then the "mare's leg"—a Winchester pump shotgun with some of the barrel professionally cut back and fitted with a special stock. It was a fierce, stubby looking thing and it had a lot of kick. His buddy Jay Jackson, an agent at DEA, sold it to him. Jay was a black guy that read a lot about the old West. He said that back then they called a man's pistol a "hog's leg", but this thing here, it was a "mare's leg." Then he told Maitland, "a mare is a horse, you see" and Maitland said, yeah, he knew that.

Maitland had been in a bad scrape a year earlier and got one of his lungs shot out. He had only had the .38 snub at that time and it probably saved his life. But if he'd had the stubby little shotgun with him he might not have lost a lung. Jay Jackson said, "This will be for those mean jobs. Where you can hit someone when you don't have time to aim." Effective, yes, but scary just to look at. Hopefully it would be enough just to let Hicks see it.

About twenty miles out of town he called Bianca from his cellphone. She didn't answer so he left a message and told her he'd be back in a couple of days and to call him if she needed anything. Probably still mad at me, he told himself. And then wondered why she should be.

He drove west into Iowa as night fell and he found a talk station on the radio to keep him company.

# PART 3
## FRIDAY

PART 2

FRIDAY

# SEVEN

The man behind the counter at the convenience store studied and ogled Nina Harrow as she approached him with her purchases. A couple of pieces of fruit, a bottle of water, a sandwich and a bag of Skittles. Blonde piece of work, early thirties, looking a little like Angie Dickinson in her policewoman days. Pretty, but kind of tough looking and serious. He took in the clothes, the Lexus, and the expensive haircut and thought, she's not from here. He could ask for her driver's license when she pulled out her credit card to pay though it would not be necessary and then he would know where she came from. Or, stop being such a pussy, and just *ask* her.

But she asked him a question.

"Excuse me?"

She pointed to the road outside.

"Will this road take me to Union City?"

"Union City? Uh, what do you want to go there for?"

The woman smiled. Not a warm smile, but a patient and confident one, telling him she'd like an answer.

"Can you tell me?" she said.

"Well, yeah. It's not the quickest way, though."

"What is?"

The clerk hesitated. The woman was pretty, a little standoffish, but she seemed like she could be nice if she wanted. He wondered if she knew what she was doing.

He said, "There's a state road four miles up. Route J. It'll take you there. But . . ."

"What?"

"What do you want to go there for?"

Nina looked at the clerk. A kid, maybe nineteen or twenty, looking at her face now instead of her chest or hips. Was he concerned or just horny? . . . *Oh, he's just a kid.*

She said, "It's family business." She thanked him and left.

The clerk looked out the window at her car as it faded out of view. He had about half fallen in love with the lady in that short space of time and now he felt a slight weight in his heart for her. He didn't quite know why, but he wished she had not come here.

The sign on the edge of town said "Union City" and under that it said the population was 4,899. The sign was in front of her and then it was behind her and she was on the main street which was called Main Street. A black and white sign said the speed limit was 25. There was a pawn-shop, a corner steakhouse, a donut shop, and the Cimmarron Valley Co-Op. Further down the road was a nine story grain elevator aged to a battleship gray that said Robin Hood Flour at the top. Railroad tracks ran up to the side of the grain elevator. Grass sprang out between the rails.

Nina Harrow had grown up in Fort Worth, Texas, and had taken the twenty-two-mile road to Dallas no more than a week after finishing high school. Fort Worth was not a small town, but it felt like one to her and she wanted to put it behind her. Now she took in the sight of Union City, Kansas, and almost said aloud, "Well, here's a place to die." Then stopped, frightened suddenly by the ugliness of her thought. Of boredom, she had meant. That's all she meant.

Across the street from the donut shop was a small, one-story building that said "Town Hall." Nina looked closer and saw a police car parked next to it. "Union City Police," it read, arcing on the doors to fit. She slowed the Lexus and made a wide turn to park diagonally in front. When she got out she saw that one side of the building was town hall while the other was the police department.

Nina opened a glass door and immediately found herself standing in front of a receptionist's counter. Then a heavy-set receptionist said, "Can I help you?" Though she hadn't gotten up from her desk. The receptionist was around fifty and looked like she had been attractive twenty years ago but somewhere along the way just said the hell with it. Nina thought of her mother and then felt a stab of guilt and self-loathing. Heard her mother saying, it must be nice to be so pretty.

Nina said, "I'd like to talk to the police chief."

The woman regarded her from behind her desk, not smiling or making it easy. She said, "Did you have an appointment?"

"No, ma'am."

"Who are you?"

"My name is Nina Harrow. I'm from Dallas. Texas."

"I know where it is. Are you selling something?"

"No. I need to talk to him about—I need to talk to him about my sister."

"Who is your sister?"

"Her name is Donna. She—listen, if I need to make an appointment to see him, can I do that through you?"

The receptionist made a point of sighing, then came out from behind the desk and walked up to the counter. "Just hold on," she said. "I'll see if he's available."

Nina watched her walk down the hall. Briefly, she considered throwing her purse at the back of the woman's head. She didn't treat people like that and she wondered why other people bothered to.

The receptionist came out of a room at the end of the hall about five minutes later and said, "He'll see you now," pointing her thumb over her back shoulder. The woman didn't even break stride as she walked past Nina and back to the safety of her desk, and Nina almost laughed at the lady's utter lack of manners.

Nina walked down the carpeted hallway, peered around the open doorway, and said hello.

A man wearing tan slacks and a white short-sleeved shirt with a badge said, "Come on in." He had not gotten out of his chair behind his desk. You're not in the South anymore, Nina thought. She glanced at the pistol clipped to a holster at his waist.

"My name is Nina Harrow."

"I'm Jason Bender. I'm the chief."

He was a stocky man, with sandy hair and spectacles. Younger than she imagined a police chief would be. His late thirties, maybe only five or six years older than her.

Nina stood there uncertainly and then Chief Bender gestured to a chair in front of the desk so she could sit.

Nina said, "I drove here from Dallas. My younger sister Donna Harrow lives here, I think. And we haven't heard from her in almost a month and we're worried about her."

"We . . ."

"My mother and I."

"And you're from Dallas . . . Texas?"

"Well, I live in Dallas. My mother lives in Fort Worth."

"Aren't they the same?"

"No."

"Your father, what about him?"

"He—he left when I was little. I don't know where he is."

Chief Bender nodded, as if to understand.

Nina said, "My mother wants me to check on her. Maybe bring her home."

"I see. What makes you think your little sister's here?"

"Well, she told us—she told my mother that she moved here about a year ago."

"Moved to Union City, Kansas?" He gestured as if to say, who would choose to do that?

"Yes."

"From where?"

"Kansas City."

"What was she doing in Kansas City?"

Nina thought the question was odd. But he was a policeman, wasn't he.

"She was there with a guy, lived there with a guy for a while. And then she met another guy and came here to live with him."

"Another guy," the chief said.

"Yes." Nina was not going to apologize for it.

"Ma'am, pardon me if I'm speaking out of turn, but was your sister something of a drifter?"

Nina frowned.

"Yes, she was."

"Has she ever been arrested?"

"I don't know," Nina said. Though she was sure Donna had.

"How old is she?"

"Twenty-six." Nina reflected. "She would have turned twenty-six ten days ago."

Chief Bender sighed.

"I apologize, ma'am, if I sound insensitive. I don't mean to be. But the thing about drifters is, they drift. Now I haven't come across Donna Harrow or heard of her. She

71

might be in California for all we know."

"If she were in California, she would have called my mother and told her she was in California."

"Ma'am, please don't get upset. But you don't know that. Do you mind if I ask you something?"

"No."

"How long has it been since *you've* seen your sister?"

Nina thought, you prick. She said, "It's been a couple of years."

He tried not to smile at his little victory.

He said, "A lot can happen to someone in that time. Especially if they've been living on the underside."

"What do you mean, sir?"

"Ma'am, I mean that when people get hooked into a substance abuse lifestyle, everything changes. It's a tragic thing, but it's the way it is."

"I never said my sister was a drug addict."

"No ma'am, you didn't say that directly. But am I right that she may be?"

After a moment, Nina said, "She may be."

Chief Bender said, "I'm sorry to hear it. If she's in trouble, I hope you find her and get her the help she needs."

"Thank you," Nina said. "She was living with a guy named Jett."

The chief said, "Excuse me?"

"She was living with a guy named Jett."

"Jett who?"

"I'm sorry, but I don't know."

The chief shook his head in disappointment.

"Ms. Harrow, I'm sorry I'm not much of a help to you. But that's really not much to go on. Now if you want to fill out a missing persons report, we can do that. Then I can forward it to state and county police, see if something turns up."

Nina said. "You'll help me with that?"

"Be happy to."

Twenty minutes later she walked out the front door. Late afternoon, chilly. Mid-March and the sky was fading pink and blue. The air was clean and it was quiet. She heard a car and then she saw it. A red Mercedes swung in and parked next to her Lexus. Briefly Nina thought of horses tethered to a rail in front of the town saloon. Silly, she thought. She wondered if it came from being in a small town or if she was just tired.

A blond haired man got out of the Mercedes. He regarded her briefly, giving her a half smile before walking into the police station.

The man did not look like her fiancé, Michael. But he made Nina think of Michael for some reason. She pictured Michael now, with his well cut hair and Polo shorts and his yellow shirt with the palm trees on it, standing by the grill in his backyard, telling their guests to get themselves a beer. Michael liked having people over. He liked to talk about sports and Warren Buffett and Darrell Royal and the guy that owned the Dallas Mavericks and all the money he had. He was a confident man, a successful junior partner at Jones Day. She liked his confidence and, yes, she liked the money. He bought her nice things and he took her on nice vacations. Michael was divorced with two children. A little boy and girl, aged six and eight, respectively. They stayed with their mother during the week, with Michael on the weekends. Which meant he and Nina were not supposed to stay the night together on the weekends. It was complicated, but she told herself that most available men were divorced with kids.

She had thought about their relationship during the drive. She believed she loved him and she wanted to be married to him. But the drive from Dallas to Kansas is a long one and there is little to see and much time to think. So somewhere along the way she speculated on how quickly they had become engaged. They met at a party he had given that she had gone to with a friend. And he had pursued her hard. He had not made a pass, had not even tried to kiss her that night. But he asked for her number and took her out for coffee that weekend. On that first date, he had told her about his divorce, how his wife had not understood him but she was a good person and they were civil to each other for the children. He had not said or done anything wrong. He was smooth and inoffensive. And soon they were calling each other almost every day and seeing each other two nights a week. They made love on their seventh date. It was quick and awkward, messy too and not in a good way. She was still dry but he was in a hurry and he rushed it and in less than a minute it was over. He did not say he was sorry, as some men do, but rolled over on his back and said, "That was great." And Nina thought, great? Are we in the same movie? The sex got better after that, but not by much. And such small portions. After a few months, she got the idea that he did not enjoy sex very much. And she thought, well, this was something her mama had not told her. It was supposed to be the man that wanted it all the time while the woman parsed it out. But it became fairly clear that Michael just . . . wasn't . . . into . . . it.

She felt bad when she thought about it. He talked nicely to her, considerate, always asking her if she needed anything. When he had his parties, he always had his arm around her. Though he did not caress her much after everyone left. But he often told her he loved her and that she meant everything to him. He was good looking, rich, and generous. She believed she would never have to worry about him leaving her or smacking her or coming home drunk. Nor would she have to worry about being poor. Which was what she had been all through her childhood.

Which was not too much to comprehend on a Sunday. But then two days before she left for Kansas, she ran into a woman who had been a friend of Michael's ex-wife. The woman was French and she had been married four times. Most of Nina's friends thought the French woman was vulgar and tacky. They spoke in the waiting area of the Estée Lauder spa at the Northpark Mall, sitting in chairs in white cotton robes while the massage therapists cleared the tables and got their oils ready.

Nina told the woman about her engagement to Michael. No, a date had not been set yet, but they were working on that. After they got conversation past the first two or three levels, the French woman said, "Michael Gunst? Michael Gunst is your fiancé?"

Nina said he was.

The French woman looked at the large engagement ring on Nina Harrow's hand.

She said, "What about the sex?"

"Excuse me?" Nina said.

The French woman said, "What about the sex?"

"I—I don't think that's any of your business."

"Oh, come on. Is the sex good?"

"I'm not answering that."

"Ach, who cares? Is not everything, sex. But it is something, no? Is it important to you?"

"—yes. Yes, it's important to me."

"Not to him, though, uh?"

"I beg your pardon."

"You know that's why his first wife left him. He did not like to fuck."

Jesus God, the French lady said it right there in the Estée Lauder waiting room. *He did not like to fuck.* Like it was something that should be put on his tombstone. Folks, the man simply did not like to fuck.

Nina's first instinct was to tell the woman to shut her French frog ass up. But she knew if the comment had been directed at someone else and she, Nina, had been there to witness it, she would have laughed pretty hard. Jesus. He did not like to *fffuque,* Frenching it up. Smart-ass bitch, trying to get a rise out of the Texas American yokel girl by shocking her. Hoping to draw a reaction from the Southern belle: *Why, I do de-clare. Such language from a lady.* Nina's next instinct was to shake her head and go back to her *Vogue* magazine.

But she was intrigued now. And after a moment, she couldn't help asking.

"How do you know that?" Nina said.

The French woman shrugged. Like, everyone knows it. Bitch. She said, "This is North Dallas." Like that explained everything.

Nina said, "He's not—"

"I'm not saying he is." The French woman said, "I'm not saying he's a homosexual, you see. I don't think he's that. He's just not a lover. Some men, it is not important to them. If you don't want a lover, then you'll be fine."

A white smocked therapist came out and led the bitch away before Nina could tell her to go fuck herself. Then she thought, no, that wouldn't be good enough. Then she thought, shit, I should have said, "You're the one that needs to get laid." That would have showed her.

But the French woman was gone, and Nina doubted she

would have had the guts to say it anyway.

Nina left without getting her massage and in the parking lot she burst into tears. Women can be so awful to each other, she thought. What did I do to her? What did I do to deserve such cruelty? It wasn't so much what the French bitch had said. It was that she seemed so sure. So—

*He does not like to fuck.*

—so right.

The words played back to her on I-35 through the cornfields and the cattle grazing on the red clay jutting out of the green rolling hills of central Oklahoma. And when she thought of the words, she wondered if the French woman was a demon or an angel. Wondered if the woman was being spiteful or if she was genuinely trying to help. Was she trying to put the cute little Texas blond in her place? Or was she trying to save a sister from the confines of a contemporary arranged marriage? One arranged not by families, but by money and social expectations and her own unacknowledged fear.

*If you don't want a lover, you'll be fine.*

God, like she didn't have enough things to worry about. Nina looked up and down the street, her hands on her hips. A block away she saw a sign that said "Cobb's Café." She walked up to it and went inside.

# EIGHT

The chief studied the mug shots for a moment then pushed them back across the desk to Maitland.

Chief Bender said, "What makes you think your boy is here?"

Maitland said, "I think he used to spend his summers here."

"He's from Chicago?"

"Yeah."

"Why come here?"

"His mother's cousin. A woman named Cora Reed. He and his brother spent a couple of summers here, probably when they were kids."

"How do you know that?"

"A newspaper article in Hicks' apartment. His brother played basketball for Kansas. The article said that Edward Hicks was from Chicago, but he used to spend his summers in Union City."

The police chief let silence fall between them, using it to his advantage before he spoke again.

"A newspaper article," Chief Bender said.

"Yes."

"And based on that, you think Thomas Hicks is here."

Maitland realized it was a question. Maitland had shown the chief a certified copy of the bail bond, the power of attorney authorizing the appropriate law enforcement agency to surrender Thomas Hicks to him. He had shown him the mug shots too. The chief just sat there, determined not to be impressed.

Maitland said, "I thought it was worth looking into."

Chief Bender said, "What do you want from me?"

"I have the address of Cora Reed's home. I'd like to ask for some help from your department."

"Why?"

"Thomas Hicks is a violent man. He's wanted for two murders. So I could use some help."

"What you're saying is, you want to put my men in the line of fire. Endanger them too?"

"That's not what I'm saying."

"This Hicks, he's not my problem."

"There's a warrant out for his arrest. You are law enforcement."

"And you've offered me no proof that he's here."

"If you believe that, your men won't be in danger."

Chief Bender tightened his face.

"Mr. Maitland, I don't want to quibble with you. But you're taking things for granted. You think you can pull into town in your Mercedes and ask us country boys to accompany you out to a farm so you can catch some boy you say is from Chicago. Well sir, we don't work for you. We work for the people of this town."

Maitland kept his voice even.

"I understand that, chief. But if Thomas Hicks is here, I would imagine the citizens of Union City would want him arrested and taken away. To my way of thinking, we're on the same page."

"The same page," the chief said. Like it was a stupid expression. "Let me ask you this: Just how much is he worth to you?"

"Pardon me?"

"What is Hicks worth to you, personally, if you catch him and get him back to Chicago?"

It took Maitland a minute to get it and when he did get it, he hoped he was wrong, hoped he had misunderstood because this man was law enforcement and Maitland did not want to be right about something like this. But he looked at the Union City police chief and he knew that he was right. And then he thought, shit. The man is dirty. He wanted a cut of Maitland's fee.

Maitland said, "Are you asking me how much I'm getting paid?"

"Yeah."

Maitland said, "Why?"

The question pushed the chief back a bit. Not so much the why, but the tone in which Maitland had said it. A distinct suggestion of corruption. Which was intended.

The chief said, "Just curious. No need to get offended."

Maitland said nothing, aware that his silence would make the chief uncomfortable. It did, too. For a brief moment they exchanged a stare that probably communicated more than the spoken words that had gone before. The chief figuring out now that the bounty hunter was not going to play.

The chief said, "I can't help you."

Maitland let himself out. He walked out the front door, telling himself to calm down. Fucking cops, he thought. Some were saints, most were just guys doing a job, and some were just assholes. But it was the assholes you remembered. It was the crooked pieces of shit like Chief Huckleberry here that stuck with you. Seeking a piece of Maitland's fee before committing any of his men to enforcing the law. He wondered now if he should have told the chief that he had been a cop himself, eight years with Chicago PD. He wondered if it would have helped any. Probably not. A guy like that would have just tried to exploit it. Or say that didn't mean shit to him. No honor among thieves, they say.

Not too goddam much among cops either, Maitland thought.

In his anger, he played out things he wanted to say to the man. And if Thomas Hicks kills someone in your town, what then, chief? What will you tell the citizens of your shithole town then? That you would have prevented it if you could, but the bounty hunter from Chicago refused to pay the required bribe? So, folks, it's really *his* fault. Asshole.

He realized in his anger that he was frightened. Because now he knew he would have to take Hicks alone. One cop shows up and a shooter may believe, with reason, that he can kill the cop and run away, leaving one dead witness behind. Show up in numbers and the shooter may weigh the odds and surrender. Criminals that weren't high or drunk could be quite rational; not nice, necessarily, but rational and willing to do what was in their best interest. So now he was alone and the chief's greed and cowardice were placing him in danger. The son of a—put it out of your mind, Evan. Put it out and get to work.

He got in the Mercedes, drove west out of town, toward the homestead of Cora Reed where he believed a killer was hiding.

# NINE

Nina felt people looking at her when she walked into the diner. Small town and she was an alien. She wondered if they could see themselves staring.

The diner had red and white checkered curtains in the window and a countertop with stools placed in front and booths offering a view of town traffic. Coca-cola advertisements from the forties and the fifties that had been put up in the nineties, selling nostalgia with chicken fried steak. Nina hated it.

There were two men and a woman sitting in one of the booths. One of the men sat alone on his side lounged into the corner with his legs up on the seat, toothpick in his mouth. He didn't look like he was in any hurry. He didn't care that Nina noticed him eying her. He was bald and his red T-shirt stretched across his thick, rubbery form. Creep, she thought. She sat at the counter and turned so that she would not have to see him anymore.

A skinny waitress with short hair and glasses took Nina's order. She looked about nineteen and she gave Nina the reverence due prom queens and newscasters. She asked Nina how she was doing and told Nina she liked her outfit and asked Nina where she got her bracelet. Nina was polite and nice because the girl was the first person in town who had shown her any sort of kindness. Though she suspected that the girl would not be so solicitous if Nina were fat and dumpy. In the strange animal kingdom of life, Nina had learned that heterosexual women were influenced by a woman's beauty at least as much by any lesbian. Or what they perceived to be beautiful. For good and for bad, it made a difference. And any time anyone gave Nina an argument on the subject, she'd tell them to watch the complex dynamics between the co-hosts of *The View* and get back to her. Nina Harrow was not a narcissist; indeed, she did not think herself very pretty. But she knew other people did and for the most part dealt with the special treatment with grace. Beauty is fleeting, her mother often reminded her. It was in the Bible and Nina could look it up if she didn't believe her.

The waitress got around to telling Nina that today's special was catfish. Nina ordered a cheeseburger and a cup of coffee.

Nina looked at the photos hanging below the shelf separating the kitchen from the restaurant counter. People dressed like grapes, bananas, apples and some guy in underwear. . . . a Halloween party twenty years ago, Fruit of the Loom underwear being the group costume. Nina thought it was a lot of work for a joke. She wanted to go home.

The waitress returned with Nina's coffee.

She said, "My name is Sadie."

Nina told Sadie her name.

Nina said, "You live here?"

"Yeah." The girl sounded apologetic.

Nina said, "I think it's a nice place." She didn't. But she felt for the girl.

Sadie said, "No you don't. It's obvious."

Nina sipped her coffee. She said, "Do you go to school?"

Sadie said, "No. I'm thinking about going to nursing school next year. In Topeka or Kansas City."

"Really?" Nina said. "I used to be a nurse."

"No."

"Really, I did."

"Wow. So . . . what, you're not one now?"

"No," Nina said. "I work for a pharmaceutical company now. Sales."

"Cool." The girl took another look at Nina's clothes, seeing how a sales rep dressed. "Does it pay good?"

Nina shrugged. "It's okay."

"Do you miss being a nurse?"

"Some things I don't miss at all," Nina said. Thinking about doctors . . . "Other things I miss."

Sadie stayed there at the counter. Nina wondered if she would forget about the food. She suspected Sadie would ask what she was doing in town, so Nina spoke first.

"Did you ever meet a girl named Donna Harrow?"

"Donna who?" Sadie said.

"Harrow."

"Donna Harrow. What does she look like?"

"She looks kind of like me. Shorter though, with darker hair."

"Is she your sister?"

"Yes."

Sadie studied Nina. "I don't think so," she said.

Nina said, "She might have come in here with a guy named Jett. Do you know him?"

"Jett. I know a guy named Jett Penley. Is that him?"

"It might be," Nina said. "Do you know how I could reach him?"

"Well, not offhand."

"But he's here."

"He's from here. He was in KCK for a while, but then he came back."

"KCK?"

"That's Kansas City, Kansas."

"Oh, oh." Nina said, "When did he come back?"

"I think about a year ago."

Nina felt her heart beat. She said, "I think that's who I'm looking for."

". . . okay . . ."

"I need to know where he lives. Listen, I'll give you money if you help me. I can give you five hundred dollars if you tell me where he lives."

Sadie was getting frightened. She said, "I—I don't know where he lives."

"But you just said—"

"—I just said he was from here. That's all."

"But you said his last name was Penley. Is that P-E-N-L-E-Y?"

"I don't know," the girl said. "I have to get back to work."

After the waitress left, Nina felt something. A ghost perhaps or some other bad force. She turned to look at the table.

The bald-headed man was staring straight at her.

The door to the Town Hall/Police Department was locked. It was after five. A small sign said to ring the doorbell if the door was locked. Nina rang the bell. Once, then twice more.

A couple of minutes later a man in a police uniform came to the door. It was not Chief Bender, but a younger policeman, maybe as young as twenty-three or twenty-four, with a name tag that said "ROKE". He wore cheap sunglasses with an orange tint and his ears stuck out.

Nina watched him as he looked her up and down, as if his sunglasses would allow him to get away with it.

Officer Roke said, "Yeah." Insolence in his voice.

Nina told him who she was and why she had been here earlier. He stared at her while she talked. He did not nod his head or give her any other sort of encouragement.

So Nina said, "Well, is Chief Bender here?"

"No," Roke said. "Gone home for the day."

"When I was here earlier, I didn't know my sister's boy-friend's name. But I think I know it now. I think it would help."

"Hmmm," Roke said. "You didn't know it before."

"Yes."

"But now you do."

Nina thought, fucking cop. She was asking for help, not understanding after being pulled over for speeding. Dink couldn't tell the difference.

"Yes, officer," Nina said, with a little edge. "I do."

Officer Roke looked off to his right, demonstrating that he was cool and bored in this little interrogation. "So what's his name?"

Nina said, "His name is Jett Penley."

"Who told you that?"

"Pardon me?"

"Who told you his name?"

A small alarm went off. Nina could not explain it, but she knew she felt it.

"My mother told me. I called her and she told me."

Roke seemed to stare at her through his sunglasses for a moment. Then he gave a slow nod.

Nina said, "So is that name familiar to you? I mean, do you know Jett Penley?"

"You need to speak with the chief."

"Do you need to ask the chief if you know who Jett Penley is? Or where he is?"

Something shifted in the man's stance then. His body language giving something away. Not much, but something. Like he was anxious and wanting to get back inside.

Nina said, "Can't you help me?"

"Ma'am, if it's so damn important to you, why don't you come back in the morning. Tell the chief your troubles."

He backed in the door and closed it.

"I will," Nina said, loud enough for him to hear through the glass. She said, under her breath, "Asshole."

She retreated to her car. She put the key in the ignition and then stopped.

God it would be so nice to leave. Crappy, shitty town with low life people treating her like she was stupid. A nuisance. All these television shows about a rich doctor or big city businessman coming to live in a small town to get away from the rat race and live with decent, normal people . . . it was a big bunch of shit. She had been to New York twice and was not treated so rudely. A chief of police talking to her like she was a fool and her sister was a hopeless skank best forgotten; men staring at her like she was a piece of meat . . . friendly, her ass.

Just turn the key and put this sheep-shearing trading post behind her.

Nina sat back in her seat and closed her eyes. When she opened them, she dialed a number on her cell phone.

"Hello?"

"Hi, mom. It's Nina."

Her mother did not have the same last name as Nina. She had kept the name of her second husband though they had divorced years ago. She was Barbara Covell, not Barbara Harrow.

Mrs. Covell said, "Well?"

Nina said, "I haven't found her."

Barbara Covell made a sighing sound that seemed to say, *I'm not surprised*. She said, "What have you done? Have you done anything?"

"I spoke with the chief of police. He had me fill out a missing persons report."

"And?"

"And—no one here has heard of her, Mama."

Another sigh. "So I suppose you're on your way back to Dallas now."

"No, Mama, I'm not. I'm still—"

"If you're too busy to do this—"

"Mama, I'm not too busy. It's just that—no one knows where she is." Nina looked at the clock on the dashboard. "Mama, I think we should hire a private detective."

"Now how am I going to afford that?"

"I'll pay for it."

"Oh, sure. Just write a check. It's only my daughter."

"Mama." Nina counted to five. "Listen. I'm going to stay the night here. I'll talk with the police again tomorrow."

"What good will that do?"

Jesus Christ, Nina thought. The woman cannot be pleased. Nina was about to tell her that she had just complained that Nina was leaving too soon. But she didn't get the chance.

"Just bring her home," Mrs. Covell said. Her voice cracked. "Bring her home, will you?"

"I'll try, Mama. Okay? I'll try."

Barbara Covell hung up the phone without saying goodbye. Nina sat alone in the car, contemplating it. How could you be mad at the woman? She had always liked Donna more. Probably because Donna had remained down, had remained a loser. Nina knew this was a terrible thing to believe, but she knew that she believed it. But she could not be angry with her mother. To hear her voice cracking on the phone was to understand the meaning of the expression sick with grief. Her mother had lost her little girl and she needed to know where she was. It was an awful situation and it made Nina wonder if she would slap Donna across the face if she found her for putting them both through this.

And when that thought registered, Nina Harrow felt a surge of shame that overwhelmed her. She spent the next ten minutes crying alone.

# TEN

Garrett said, "I want to make sure I understand this. You *told* her to come back in the morning?"

Teddy Roke said, "No, Garrett. What I said was, if it's so important to you, why don't you come back in the morning."

Jason Bender said, "How's that different?"

Roke stood in the gravel parking lot of Wood Used Truck and Equipment Sales. There were some prefabricated steel buildings that looked like miniature barns on the lot and double carports on sale, $595 installed. A white VW Beetle sat near the side, its roof rusted brown.

It was Garrett's place of business.

Roke had thought it might be easier to tell them about the woman here as opposed to the station where the chief would have the advantage of questioning him from behind his desk. He realized now that he had been wrong, Garrett staring at him coldly. Roke thought, discipline, my ass; he's thinking about blowing my head off.

He glanced at Chief Bender, hoping for some sort of gesture of reassurance. None was there. Shit.

Roke had known Jason Bender since he—Roke—was a kid. For a good deal of his life, he had thought of Bender as just some guy his older brother had gone to high school with. Just some dude, kind of stocky, but no one to be particularly scared of. Then Jason was a cop and later he became chief. Bender became chief after the previous chief got drunk, ran a stop sign and killed two kids making a left turn onto the highway. Jason and Garrett persuaded the families of the kids to sue the chief and run him out of office. They would later say they had encouraged the lawsuit because it had been the right thing to do, but no one in the department believed they had any other motive than to become chief and assistant chief, respectively. After the families settled their claims, Jason bought ten acres north of town. Part of his consultation fee for the lawyer he had referred the case to.

It was Jason Bender that hired Roke as a police officer. At the time, Jason had told him, "Ted, I don't know about you. On the one hand, I think you could be an excellent law enforcement officer. On the other hand, you've got some things in your past that concern me. Statutory rape and a VPO from your first wife. What have you got to say about that?" Roke had responded that, yes sir, he had made some mistakes in the past, but he was mature now and he had always wanted to work in law enforcement and that he would do whatever it took to get the job done. Jason Bender said, all right, he would take a chance on him. But he needed to remember who his friends were.

Standing on the ground before the chief and his assistant, Roke was scared and he wondered if they were his friends.

Roke said, "Boys, I—I didn't bring her here."

Garrett said, "What the hell's that supposed to mean?"

Roke swallowed. "Nothing, Garrett. I just—I didn't mean nothing by that."

Chief Bender said, "All right, let's everybody just calm down." He said, "The thing is, she's here."

Garrett Wood said, "Yeah, she's here. So what?"

Bender said, "So what?" He shook his head, like Garrett was slow or something. "She's looking for her sister, Garrett."

"Shit," Garrett said. "Do you know how many crank

whores disappear each year? The woman's a statistic."

"Have you been listening?" Bender said. "What'd I just tell you?"

Garrett said, "You said the woman's asking questions around town about Jett. Yeah, I heard you, Jason. But, tell me, what has she found out?"

Bender said, "She found out Jett Penley's name. That turd's got family in this county. What if she talks to them?"

"They're not gonna say anything because they don't know anything."

"Maybe not," Bender said. "But this woman ain't the Penleys. She doesn't have to live here. You see my point? She's not afraid of us."

Garrett Wood said, "What are you afraid of?"

Bender smiled.

He said, "Garrett, put it back in your pants. We got a problem here. And if we don't take care of it, this woman may come back with federal agents. Or the KBI. You understand that?"

Garrett Wood and Jason Bender looked at each other. Men who had sworn oaths to uphold the law, staring at each other and not sure what to do next. Both of them frightened but not willing to admit it. They lived in a rural area rife with methamphetamine labs—the moonshine of the twenty-first century. Somewhere, somebody believed that you could eliminate the scourge of illegal narcotics with effective law enforcement, but these two had stopped believing it long ago. You can declare war on it and search cars and homes and bend and maybe even break the rules of search and seizure, but you were no more going to stop the drug trafficking than you were going to stop the rain from falling. And if it was going to fall on the just and the unjust, you might just as well get a piece of it.

Like most parties to a corrupt relationship, each had something on the other. Bender knew that Garrett and his brother weren't just selling used trucks and equipment. They were selling meth. But the Wood Brothers had been paying Bender protection money—a share of the profits to leave them alone. In those rare moments when he was honest with himself, Jason would admit that he had probably always known what the Wood brothers were up to. Any police officer would know Carl Wood to be a turd just to look at him. But it was too late to do anything about it now. Chief Bender had saved some of the money, but spent a lot of it. A boat, new furniture for his wife, an addition to the house . . . if you were married with a family, it always seemed to go somewhere. Besides, Jason would think, what did it matter what a man did out here, in a prairie as empty and as vast as the desert? Who cared?

Bender said it again. "Do you understand, Garrett?"

Garrett said, "I understand as well as you."

Bender sighed and nodded some sort of communication. It would begin now and there would be no turning back.

Garrett said to Roke, "She staying the night here?"

"Yes, sir. At the Lincoln Hotel."

"Go on back," Garrett said. "Tell Russell to get over there and to let us know if she tries to leave. Roke. Tell Russell he is not to touch her, unless he hears it from me. Is that clear?"

"Yes, sir."

Roke got into his patrol car and swung out of the lot, crunching gravel until he hit the road.

Garrett said, "We can take her from the hotel."

Bender said, "And bury her outside of town. That all you got?"

"What else is there?"

93

Bender shook his head. "Then we'll have more family. Or her husband or boyfriend coming up here. I've seen the woman. She's the kind of woman that people miss. Good people."

Garrett said, "I'm open to suggestions."

Bender was pleased with Garrett's deference. But it delegated the decision back to him, and usually he didn't need that. But this time, it was okay.

Chief Bender said, "We could do it in a way that we wouldn't have to hide her. We wouldn't have to hide it."

"I'm not following you."

"If she were killed by a felon. A felon on the run from the law."

Garrett Wood smiled. He said, "You know where we can find one?"

Chief Bender said, "Sometimes you get lucky."

The chief was smiling now too.

# ELEVEN

The county road arced into a full right turn amidst the landscape of the plains. Yellow, green, and brown. It was pretty country. Maitland drove another half-mile before he slowed the car. Then stopped.

On his left were two dilapidated wooden structures, sitting abandoned in the tall grass. Up and to the north was a concrete structure about the size of an outhouse. Between the wood and concrete structures was a narrow dirt road that sloped off the county road. The dirt road sank down among high grass ledges with trees branches draping over, forming something of a tunnel.

It was a good place for an ambush, Maitland thought. A man could place himself behind one of those trees and pick a rider off his horse with a deer rifle. Like the French and the Indians had to ambush George Washington's men, back when Washington was fighting for the British. Silly to think of that now, he thought. But he thought it anyway and trusted his instinct to survive.

Maitland parked the Mercedes behind the wooden shacks. He took his stubby shotgun and a pair of binoculars and began walking toward the Reed house, keeping the narrow dirt road well to his right. As he walked, he was conscious of country sounds. Birds and critters and wind and, beyond that, quiet. He was a creature of the city, and he was aware that the absence of traffic and bustle could disorient him, make him feel anxious even.

It was a nice view. In the distance the land went down

and flattened out into a valley that must have once given hope and joy to an immigrant settler. Stretching out to the western horizon, Colorado and all the way to California if you were feeling ambitious.

Maitland walked until he came up on a line of trees. He stepped up to them carefully and then found that he was at the top of a ridge that overlooked the house.

Leaving the car behind had been a good idea. The dirt road that came off the highway would have taken him right to the front of the house. If Hicks were inside, he would have heard the car and taken evasive action. Or hostile action; gotten a gun and started plugging holes in the car's windshield.

The house was small and blue. To the front and beyond the house, there was a steel gray garage with three open bays. There was a green tractor and a red Chevy pick up inside. Next to the house, closer to Maitland's perch, there was an empty horse trailer.

There were no vehicles with Illinois license tags.

Well, Maitland thought, no one said Hicks had to make it easy. Leave a sign outside with a big arrow that says, "He's in here." Hicks had not agreed to be dumb. And if he was not here and the entire trip had been a waste of time, so be it.

Maitland looked up, east and west. About thirty minutes of daylight left. If Hicks was home, he would know the house better in the dark than Maitland would. But if it were light, Hicks might see him coming outside. Risky either way, but riskier to do it in daylight. Maitland looked through the binoculars at the windows. He did not see anyone. After scoping it out, he decided that the ridge was too steep to descend and it was too exposed to the front of the house. He would circle around and come up to the back.

When the sun set, that's what he did.

It's not an easy thing to sneak up on a house. You can imagine you're the predator, moving in on your prey. But the people inside may have seen you coming a mile away and may be armed and ready and licking their lips, waiting for you to walk into it. Maitland remembered, when he had been a patrolman, getting a call on a shooting. A couple of young wolves had made a tidy sum on home invasions. What they would do is go down the street of a suburb with a remote control garage door opener, aim and shoot until they found a door with the right frequency. When the garage door opened, they would go through that door and then through the door to the home. Go in with guns drawn, terrorize the homeowners and steal all the cash and jewelry. They never took anything they couldn't fit in their pockets. They were young guys—big and fearsome. They made the news and got some moderate fame. One night, they hit a house in Mount Prospect and an old man with a television, a frontiersman's instinct, and a 1911 .45 was ready right after he heard the garage door open. There was a small utility room separating the garage from the rest of the house. The first home invader had just opened the second door when the old man shot him twice in the chest. The second home invader turned to run but the old man put one in his back anyway. Both of the home invaders died. The urban liberals scowled, the neighbors quietly cheered, and the District Attorney did not file charges against the old man. Maitland remembered squatting down and examining the two dead men on the floor while the old man asked him if he'd like a Coke or something, like Maitland was there to fix the washing machine.

Thomas Hicks was young and quick and he'd killed two men already.

Maitland took a long arc and came up behind the house in the dark. He walked through the yard, stepping carefully, waiting to hear the rack slide on a handgun or some indication that someone was about to shoot him. Though he knew if he were to be shot he'd never hear it. When the shot that kills you comes, you never hear it first, you're just dead when a second earlier you had been alive.

When he got closer to the house, he could see light emanating from the windows. Slowly, very slowly, he stepped up to the back door, hunched over then straightening up as he peered through the door's window inside. No one he could see. He could hear, though, the faint murmur of a television. Okay, someone is watching television and hopefully he would keep his attention there.

Maitland faced the house. In his right hand, he held the shotgun by its stock, his index finger resting ahead of the trigger, the barrel pointing to the ground. With his left hand, he gripped the handle of the screen door. He pulled, just.

A creak. Just perceptible, but perceptible. Maitland held his breath and eased the door back into place. It would make too much noise and, if unlucky, give the man inside time to get to a gun. He did not want a gunfight. He wanted all the advantages he could get. He walked around to the west side of the house, edging along until he found a window that was not lighted. He looked inside the window, peered in and let his eyes adjust to the darkness of the room. It was unoccupied. Good. He placed the shotgun against the side of the house. Then he slowly slid the window up. He picked up the shotgun and crawled in.

Once in, he felt his heart pounding, could feel it thrumming his ears. He was in someone's house now, breaking and entering if you wanted to get technical about it. They could shoot him and claim self-defense—*Bounty hunter? How was I to know that?*—and they'd be on solid ground too. He was in someone's house now without any positive assurance that the skipper was there. But it was too late to think about things like that. He was in now and he would have to see it through.

There were twin beds in the room and a little table with a lamp on top between. The beds were made. It smelled like a room in a grandmother's house. Maitland crossed the room and turned the knob on the door. He peered through the crack he made in the door, then opened it and stepped out into the hallway.

There was no one there.

He could hear the television better now. Cheers, muffled roars. A sporting event, taking place indoors, not outdoors. Maitland stepped down the hallway where the light from a parlor spilled into the end of the hall. He peered around a corner and saw the television. If the TV sees, he thought, it sees me. He looked back from the television and saw a black man sitting in a chair, his eyes focused on the screen.

Jesus. It was him. It was Thomas Hicks.

Maitland thought, I knew it. His ego satisfied.

And now for the rest.

Maitland stepped out of the shadow of the hall, into the room, both hands on the shotgun now as he raised it to the level of his waist, the muzzle pointed at the man in the chair.

"Hey," Maitland said.

Hicks turned sharply, surprise showing in his face.

Maitland said, "Show me your hands."

Hicks did it, though not immediately. He was trying to process it, the sudden appearance of this white man pointing a sawed off shotgun at him disorienting him. Cop, maybe.

But he was not in uniform. So maybe it was one of those Aryan heartland motherfuckers likes to kill federal agents and niggers. The guy had blond hair, if that meant anything.

Hicks said, "What do you want?" Putting some command in his tone, in spite of himself.

"Mr. Hicks, my name is Maitland. I work for Charlie Mead."

Hicks processed that too. He almost seemed to smile. Either out of admiration or shock or his own bad luck. Maybe relief, too, though, because it wasn't a Timothy McVeigh wannabe coming to show him what they did to boys like him in Kansas.

"You a bounty hunter?"

"Yep."

"You don't look like one."

"No? Who were you expecting, Tex Cobb?"

"Cobb? . . . Is he that boxer, got his ass whooped by Larry Holmes?"

"That's him."

Hicks frowned. "Now why would I expect him?"

"Because he looks like a bounty hunter. People tell me I look like a schoolteacher."

"Do they now?" Hicks gave Maitland a smile that said, don't blow smoke at me. He said, "Who you looking for?"

"Thomas Hicks."

"Hicks, huh? I ain't seen him."

"I have. I've got photos in my car. Mugshots. They're of a guy that looks an awful lot like you."

"Maybe we all look alike to you."

"Yeah, and maybe you all know Charlie Mead. Maybe you all know that Charlie Mead would have a reason to hire a bounty hunter." Maitland nodded toward the television. "Maybe you all watch the Bulls on television."

"That? That don't mean I'm from Chicago. I like the team."

"Jordan retired," Maitland said. "Who else but a Chicagoan would watch anymore?"

"I would."

"Well, you're coming with me anyway. If it turns out I'm wrong, you can sue me."

"Maybe I'll do worse than that," Hicks said.

Maitland thought, there we go. The threat. It was part of it, whether or not you looked like Tex Cobb. You could start shouting and make your head hurt, but that usually didn't do any good. Sometimes you could ignore it. But sometimes you couldn't and it was better for the skipper to know where they stood and where they might fall. Otherwise someone would get hurt.

Maitland said, "Mr. Hicks, I've killed men before. Can't say I enjoyed it, but I didn't *mind* doing it either, if you get my drift. You want to die like a warrior tonight, you can. You want to go home standing straight and take your chances with a trial, you can do that too. I'm getting paid either way."

Hicks kept his hands raised. He stood up, taking it easy, his eyes on the stubby barrel of the shotgun. He believed the man would shoot him, and he knew the man had made a point of giving him respect. Regular politician.

"Okay," Hicks said. "Just don't push me."

Maitland turned him around and cuffed his hands behind his back. After it was done, he got pissed off because Hicks said something he didn't like.

"The men you killed," Hicks said, "were they black or white?"

"I don't remember," Maitland said. "What color were the men you killed?"

# TWELVE

"Oooh," Hicks said, "I seem to have touched a nerve."

Maitland turned him back around and said, "Sit down for a minute."

"Why?"

"Because I need to sit down. Rest a bit."

The men sat across from each other, doing it slowly and with caution. Maitland's blood was up, the fear and the adrenalin leaving him and leaving him momentarily exhausted. It happens to people after they make arrests or give speeches in public.

Hicks said, "Isn't that what you want?"

"Excuse me?"

"Brothers killing brothers. Isn't that what the police want?"

"I don't know. I'm not a policeman."

Hicks regarded the bounty hunter.

"Did you used to be?"

"Yep."

"What'd you say your name was?"

"Maitland."

Hicks leaned forward, studying the man in front of him.

Maitland said, "Something wrong?"

Hicks said, "I heard a story once. About a cop with blond hair, very white boy, used to set up buys. Turned out he was a policeman working undercover. You ever hear of him?"

"No. Sounds fascinating."

"Yeah, they say he didn't look like much. Didn't look

like a cop, I mean. But as I understand it, he killed a boy named Ronnie. Ronnie Ellis, that is."

Maitland held the man's gaze.

"Yeah?" Maitland said.

"Yeah. Maybe he look like a schoolteacher too. Maybe when he was younger, he look like a punk kid, dropped out of school."

Maitland shrugged. This was not a dumb man, Maitland thought, whoever he was. Maitland saw where it was going, but he wasn't going to show the guy he was upset about it. Not by a damn sight.

"Yeah," Hicks said, smiling now. "That was you, wasn't it?"

"Yeah. That was me," Maitland said. His expression made it clear that he was not sorry about it either.

Hicks said, "Hmmm."

"Hmmm, you say. Do you disapprove?"

"I didn't say that."

"Was Ronnie a friend of yours?"

"I knew him," Hicks said.

Actually, he knew the man's sister. Sheila Ellis. She had been his girl for a short time, but he moved on before her brother had been killed. By this man. Wow. The man had killed Ronnie Ellis and Ronnie had been respected. Liked too. Ronnie was all right, for the most part.

Maitland said, "How well did you know him?"

It surprised Hicks, this question.

"I don't know. Not that well, I guess."

"I got a feeling," Maitland said, "I knew him better than you."

Hicks looked at the man again.

The way the bounty hunter said it, you could almost think he liked Ronnie. It could mean that Ronnie was a very

103

bad person and if you knew him well you would understand why his death was a positive thing. But that was not how it sounded when the bounty hunter spoke of him. The man had not said something like, "Fuck him, he was a drug dealing scumbag", which was the way most white cops talked. It was a method they used to convince themselves that homeboys weren't quite human so fucking up their livelihoods and shooting them dead was perfectly okay. Deal drugs and they get to declare war on you; that way, they can just kill you like you're a soldier wearing the enemy's uniform and not bother arresting you or dealing with you like a man. If you were a black man, your color was your uniform. It made it easy for the policemen. They wouldn't call you nigger. Not to your face, anyway. Not in these enlightened days. But substitute the word "niggers" for "drugs" and you got the general idea. "Drugs" are ruining our neighborhoods. "Drugs" are the scourge of our society. "Drugs" are responsible for most of the crime in our streets.

Hicks wondered how this man saw it. *You could ask him,* Hicks thought. *You could ask him what really happened between him and Ronnie.*

Yeah, you could ask him. But he looked like the kind of man who wasn't going to explain it to you.

Hicks said, "You taking me back to Chicago tonight?"

"Yeah."

"Can I go to the bathroom?"

"When we get on the road. We'll stop at a gas station or something."

"Why not here?"

"Because you might have a gun hidden in your bathroom."

Hicks seemed to accept this.

He said, "How did you know I'd be here?"

"You used to spend your summers here. Right?"

"Okay," Hicks said. "But I never told anyone that. How did you know?"

"A hunch."

"A hunch? Come on man, tell me."

Maitland leaned back in his chair. He did not mind the questions. Hicks seemed pretty smart though; Maitland held on to the shotgun in case the fellah was trying to get him to drop his guard and rush him.

Maitland said, "You left a newspaper clipping in your apartment. Your brother's basketball tournament."

Hicks turned his head, curious.

Maitland said, "It said that Edward used to spend his summers here. The local Kansas angle."

"Oh."

Hicks was a man of strength, but something passed across his eyes then and Maitland thought of the young man cut down on a street corner in Chicago, killed for no good reason. Christ, it could be a hard world.

"For what it's worth," Maitland said, "I'm told he was a good guy."

"Yeah," Hicks said. "He was the good one." A hint of bitterness in his tone. Which Maitland thought he understood, but didn't quite.

Hicks was thinking, yeah, the good one. White people had liked Edward and he had liked them. Like Charles Barkley, but then, not like Charles. Whites were always so proud of themselves when they could praise a "good" black. Especially when they performed such impressive 'thletic feats. *Me, a racist? Whaddaya, whaddaya? Why, my son loves Michael Jordan. He's got a great big poster of him in his room. 'Course, Michael Jordan's done something with his life; he's not just some bunny selling drugs on a street corner.*

Thomas used to say things like that to his brother, using a Richard Pryor-like white-guy voice. Teasing his little brother, but laying it on pretty hard. Edward would say Thomas didn't understand. There were good people and bad people on both sides. Edward said there was another world outside the projects if you cared to look. Thomas would say back, "You running for congress, boy?" He could almost make Edward cry when he razzed him; the boy so easy to work up. Edward.

Maitland said, "You all right?"

"I'm fine," Hicks said, angry at the question.

Maitland said, "Let's get moving. You got a coat?"

They got out to the front porch and just closed the door behind them when they heard tires whirring down the dirt road, saw light thrown up on the trees to their left, then saw two vehicles turn in and stop about twenty yards in front of them.

Police cars. No sirens or cherries flashing, but a spotlight was on both of them and the sound of a shotgun being racked. Four or five men there and one of them called out, "PUT YOUR HANDS IN THE AIR, MOTHERFUCKERS!"

That was how cops talked, Maitland thought. He knew it because he used to talk like that himself and sometimes still did if he thought it would subdue someone enough to comply with what he called "safety commands." But standing on the front porch out in the middle of nowhere with shotguns and pistols trained on him, he was not feeling much of a kinship with these boys. He was feeling scared.

Hicks said, "You bring these boys here?"

"No," Maitland said, "I did not."

After a moment, Hicks said, "I believe you. But I wish I didn't."

# THIRTEEN

Nina sat upright in the hotel room bed. The room was low budget and depressing. A brown and white room with a stale smell that you didn't want to think too much about. On the wall, there was a cheap painting of ships at sea, green swirls looking like they had been done very quickly. Like the place wasn't even trying. The television was on—CNN—but the sound was muted.

Nina was on her cell phone, getting nowhere.

Michael said, "Why don't you just come home?"

Nina said, "You think I want to be here?"

Michael sighed, again. He said, "You spoke to the police, right?"

"Yes. I told you I did."

"Well, don't get mad at me."

"I'm not getting mad at—dammit, Michael, I told you, I spoke to the chief of police. You keep acting like I didn't do it right."

"I'm just saying—"

"You're saying that if you were here, you would have handled it better."

"Nina, I did not say that. What I said was," Michael stopped, thinking of some lawyer bullshit diplomatic way of telling her she had mucked it up, "I just don't know if you presented it properly."

Jesus, Nina thought. Very smooth, Michael. Very smooth.

She said, "Well, maybe I shouldn't have spent the whole time in his office crying."

"Is that what you did?"

"No! God, do you think I'm retarded?"

"Well, you're the one that said it."

"I was kidding. God."

Nina looked at the television. A snowstorm in Boston. A foot of snow. Cars sliding around the interstate in white and grey.

She was upset. He was right about that. But not in a way the man seemed to understand. Upset, he seemed to think, because she had not *handled* the police chief properly. She had screwed it up, you see, as women will do. Probably handled it like it was one of these sorority tea parties and now she was taking it out on her clear-thinking, rational boyfriend. Nina thought, if he gives me one more of those patronizing sighs, I'm driving straight home to kick him in the balls.

Nina closed her eyes, opened them.

In a quieter voice, she said, "Michael?"

"Yes?"

"It's my sister."

"What? Oh, I know. I know, babe."

No, Nina thought, you don't. You don't understand at all. You're just saying it because you think I want to hear it. And on comprehending that, she suddenly felt that she no longer had the energy to be angry at him. He acted like he meant well and maybe for him that was good enough. But her sister was in trouble and to Michael it was a nuisance that threatened to interfere with a party he had planned for the next weekend. She could tell him he was self-centered, but then he would pull his lawyer shit and start trying to "persuade" her that he was not. Not talking like a lover, but arguing a case: proposition 1: I gave you flowers; proposition 2: I took you out for an expensive dinner last weekend;

proposition 3: . . . stick your flowers up your ass.

"Michael, I have to go. I'm very tired. I'll call you tomorrow, okay?"

"Okay, babe. . . . Okay. I love you."

"I love you too," Nina said. "Goodnight."

Clicked off the phone and shook her head, partly at her own dishonesty.

Nina aimed the remote control at the television and turned it off. She wanted the comfort of silence for a moment. She wanted the loneliness of being alone rather than the loneliness of what could be an empty relationship. Time to think about things or think about nothing at all. No such thing as the perfect man, they said. But, ssshee-it.

She went into the bathroom and washed her face. The water moistened her hairline, making the blond brown. She put the towel to her face and dried it. Then she heard the pounding on the door.

It startled her, and she went toward it with some trepidation.

"Who is it?"

"Miss Harrow? It's Chief Bender."

Nina opened the door a crack, leaving the chain on.

She saw Chief Bender through the opening. Behind him was the police officer she had seen earlier. The one with the sunglasses, only he was not wearing them now.

Nina said, "What is it?"

"We think we may have found your sister. We've got someone north of town; but she won't tell us who she is."

"She's alive?"

"Yes, ma'am. She's alive," the chief said. "But she's scared. I think it would help if she saw you. Will you come with us?"

"Let me get my coat."

She shut the door behind her and they walked toward the chief's car. A slick back with no lights on top. Bender made a head gesture to Roke and Roke got in the back seat. Nina got in the front, next to the chief. The chief started the car then slipped it out onto the county road.

The men didn't say anything; their silence puzzled Nina. She said, "So how did you find her, this woman, I mean?"

Chief Bender turned to look at her. His expression was blank.

He said, "Pardon me?"

"How—"

Roke grabbed her from behind, his left arm encircling her throat, pulling her back and pinning her against the seat. With his right hand he put the chloroformed cloth over her mouth and nose. She fought it for a few moments before she passed out.

When he was sure that she was unconscious, Bender pulled the car off to the side of the road and turned it around.

"Get her purse," Bender said. "The keys to her car are probably in there."

"Yeah?" Roke said, not understanding.

"We need her car, Ted. You're gonna drive it back."

The chief sounded irritated when he said it. He was too, because he had gone over this with Roke already. God almighty, you had to tell the boy everything twice.

# FOURTEEN

Russell peered over his shotgun at Garrett Wood, his expression a question. Garrett was the assistant chief, senior officer here. In fact, he was the only full-time police officer here. Russell, Carl Wood, and Larry Ferguson were all reserves. Garrett had known them for most of his life. Russell and Larry were the classic cop wannabes, but wouldn't make it through any certified academy. They both had records; they both liked to handle guns and rough people up. Carl had never pretended to want to be in law enforcement. Russell and Larry in uniforms now, Carl wearing his black jeans and T-shirt.

The question in Russell's mind was over the white man standing on the porch next to Hicks. Who was he and what was he doing here and what were they going to do about him?

Garrett Wood was in command and he had to put them at ease.

Garrett gestured to Russell to be cool. He called out to the white man in the anorak.

"You there, in the blue coat. Are you the bounty hunter, from Chicago?"

"Yeah," the man answered. "This man is my prisoner. Who are you guys?"

"Union City police. We'll take him from here."

Maitland said, "Why?"

Garrett was aware of his men watching him. Fucker pushing him. "He's in our jurisdiction. That's all you need to know."

Maitland said, "I spoke to your chief this afternoon. He said he wasn't going to give me any assist. So I came out here alone. Turns out, I could do it by myself."

"Well ain't that cool," Carl said.

Maitland said, "There is a warrant for this man's arrest in Cook County, Illinois. He's committed no crime in Kansas."

Garrett said, "How would you know?"

"You got a warrant?" Maitland said.

Garrett Wood looked to the men around him, three of them still training guns on Hicks, and now, Maitland. Garrett Wood said, "I don't need one."

Hicks spoke so that only Maitland could hear him. "Maitland," he said, "something's wrong. I didn't do nothing here. Not even a speeding ticket."

Maitland thought of his meeting with the chief, the chief angling for a bribe. Maitland wouldn't play, and now these guys had been sent out to collect ... was that it? Seeing four men looking ready to gun him down in the dark, he hoped that was all it was.

"Hey, man," Maitland called out, "I'm law enforcement, like you. This man is in handcuffs. Why don't you have your men lower their guns? We're on the same side."

Carl snorted. But Garrett thought things over and after a moment said, "Okay, boys."

Hicks, his voice a harsh whisper, said, "Maitland, what are you doing?"

Maitland said, "Do you know these guys?"

"No."

"Goddammit, Hicks. Don't lie to me. What have you done?"

"I didn't do a goddamn thing. You're going to get me killed, you stupid bastard."

Maitland was going to answer, but then Garrett Wood

called out. "Easy," Garrett said, his hands raised. He had put his gun in its holster. He walked over to them, then gestured for Maitland to speak to him alone. Maitland walked a short distance away from Hicks.

"Garrett Wood," he said, introducing himself. "I'm the assistant chief of Union City police. I'm sorry about all this. We're a little jumpy." Wood lowered his voice. "A woman was killed here today. Raped and murdered. This guy fits the description."

Maitland said, "Hicks?"

"Yes, sir."

"Rape and murder?"

"Yeah," Wood said. "It's bad."

"Oh."

"I didn't want to say anything in front of him. Get him spooked, you understand."

Maitland frowned, wondering if it made sense.

Maitland said, "You arresting him?"

"We're not one hundred percent sure it's him. But he fits the description. We've got a witness down at the police station. She may be able to identify him."

Maitland looked past Wood toward the three men by the police cars. Scrubby, mean-looking crew. One of them not even in a uniform, looking like someone they had pulled out of county lock-up, taken the cuffs off of, and given a gun.

Wood said, "Look, I know you got a job to do. I understand that. Why don't you come into town with us? If Hicks is the wrong guy, we'll turn him over to you and you can get on home. I know you don't want to stay here any longer than you have to."

You got that right, Maitland thought.

"All right," Maitland said. Though he didn't feel good about it.

Wood said, "Where's your vehicle?"

"It's up at the top of the driveway—I mean the road. Behind one of those shacks."

Garrett Wood looked back at his men. Maitland watched the man in the black shirt—the one not in uniform—nod to the assistant chief, something being exchanged there. He would think about that later.

"Okay," Maitland said. He walked back to Hicks.

"You're going to have to go with them," Maitland said.

For a moment, Hicks didn't say anything. He just looked at Maitland, waiting for the man to explain it.

Hicks said, "Why?"

"They have to check something out," Maitland said. He felt lame saying it.

"What are you doing to me?"

"Christ, Hicks. This is the twenty-first century. They're not going to lynch you. We're all going to the police station in town."

"You're a liar. Worse than that, you're a fool. These guys are going to do something wicked. Can't you see that?"

"How do you know that?"

"Because I know, man. *I know* I haven't given them any reason to grab me. I know it and they know it. You're the only one that doesn't know."

"Hicks, what do you want me to do? Have a shoot out with four officers of the law 'cause you got a bad feeling?"

Assistant Chief Wood came back with a bald headed cop. The bald-headed cop grabbed Hicks by the arm.

"Maitland, *Maitland,* listen to me. These men are up to something, you understand? You let them take me, I ain't gonna be alive by morning."

"Let's go boy."

"Don't you call me boy, you bald-headed cracker."

"All right," Maitland said. "All right."

The moment passed and the bald-headed cop led Hicks away.

Wood said, "Okay, then. We'll see you back at the station." He turned to leave and Maitland stopped him.

"Wood."

Garrett Wood looked at him.

"Yeah?"

Maitland said, "I don't want to see him mistreated, understand?"

Garrett Wood looked at Maitland again. Irritated at first; this outsider telling him how to do his job, but Wood was curious too. Then he smiled, like he was amused.

"You won't," Wood said.

The men got into the patrol cars; Maitland heard a couple of them laugh and felt a slight stab. The engines turned and the cars disappeared from view.

Maitland was alone.

Hicks was crazy, he thought. Dead by morning, Jesus. Where did that come from? How could he know something like that? He said he knew, but how could he know? Okay, a cracker cop had called him "boy." Maitland had heard worse than that at Chicago PD. Far worse. Every police department had its bullies. But even good cops could rough up a suspect if motivated. Particularly if there was a suspicion of murder. The blood gets up; you've seen a dead body, mutilated innocents, and you want the perp in jail. Or worse. It was a human reaction. It didn't mean you were a savage or a Klansman.

Alone in the darkness, Maitland wondered why he should feel anxious.

*You're the only that doesn't know.*

115

Convicts could be such great liars. Look at Charles Manson, one of the wiliest conmen ever to foul the earth. Talked upper class girls into cutting people to pieces. You're the only one that doesn't know. Fuck you, buddy. Know what?

Maitland decided he would feel better once he got to the police station. Out of the dark, lonely country night and under the harsh lights of civilization. Hicks in a cell and not out in some field where they could . . . Stop it. Stop thinking that horseshit; he's working you like a sociology coed in a tight sweater. The guy's killed two men in Chicago and don't forget it.

Maitland turned to look at the house behind him. The house didn't tell him anything and he started forward, to the narrow drive leading up to the shack where he'd left his car.

It was darker there, only the star shine to see by. He heard his steps and his eyes adjusted to the darkness and he saw the bluffs on both sides that had concerned him earlier. Kiowas perched up above, armed with Winchesters, waiting to shoot the Man of the Great Lakes Country. Maitland smiled; it seemed really dumb now. Now it was more complicated.

He felt better when he reached the top and saw his Mercedes. Comforted by familiar material goods, something from back home. He opened the door and placed the shotgun on the floor behind the front seat. He was standing there when he heard the car approach. Looked as lights came into view and it came closer. A police car.

It slowed and turned into the road then stopped about twenty yards in front of him.

Two men got out. The bald cop wearing the uniform top with blue jeans and the guy in the black shirt that looked like a biker.

Maitland said, "What's up?"

Carl Wood said, "We forgot to tell you something."

# FIFTEEN

Maitland had worked undercover narcotics before and he had been a police officer for several years. He had not met Carl Wood before this night. But in a way, he had. He'd met hundreds of Carl Woods. Turds, losers, douche bags, and so forth: the typical cop classifications. Looking at the drawn look of the man and his skin condition, Maitland thought, bump monkey. Meth users always looking for the "bump," the crank high. Bump monkeys. Or tweakers. Carl Wood cultivated the bad-ass look too; tattoos on the arms that he probably got in the penitentiary.

But you're not in Chicago anymore, Maitland thought. You're in Kansas. And this bad ass was sitting behind the wheel of a police car. When Kansas was younger, it was not so easy to tell the crooks from the cops because they switched sides so often. The man that robbed a bank in Logan County in June could be wearing a badge in Dodge City the next fall. A bloody frontier then. But what about now? The bleeding was supposed to have stopped in the nineteenth century after the sociopathic James brothers and Quantrill's Raiders were buried. Now it was a state with gentle, rolling lands and red and green combines cutting wheat out of the amber waves; clean fresh-looking, blonde haired girls wearing KU sweatshirts. Right?

Yeah, well . . . maybe, Maitland thought. But then there was this bad-ass with his shit-eating grin, sitting in a police car. Trouble.

Maitland said, "What is it you forgot to tell me?"

"Remember when the nigger said he'd be dead by morning?" Carl said. "Well, he was right."

Maitland reached, but Carl had a nine millimeter out the car window already and shot Maitland twice in the midsection, the bullets thunking holes into his anorak and knocking him off his feet. Maitland fell and rolled down the hill behind him. He rolled, not being able to control his fall, heard himself grunt involuntarily as he tumbled down, disoriented, with the breath knocked out of him, his body still feeling the punches the bullets had made. He kept tumbling. Then he stopped.

Maitland heard voices.

They were coming.

Maitland found it. It was in the pocket of his anorak. The .38 snubnose Chief's Special with a two-inch barrel. Short, short barrel. Not made for long distance shooting. Good for shooting a mugger in an elevator or across the width of an alley, but not good for distance. If you concentrated real hard, you could hit a target at twenty yards and get a respectable grouping. In good light, that is. In the dark? Forget about it.

And it was dark now. The shotgun sitting comfortably in his car, behind the men coming down to kill him.

"He's down there, Carl. Down there. Did you get him?"

"Hell, yes. I got him."

Jesus.

Maitland saw them, shadowy figures in the dark standing at the top of the hill like demons.

Maitland turned his body so that he faced up the hill directly. He pressed himself into the ground. He held the .38 at his side.

He kicked away the snake of panic creeping toward him and concentrated on living. He thought and made himself think—*they don't know.*

They don't know and I do know and that's the only power I have; it may not be all I need but it's all I have, the only edge I have, the only thing that will keep me alive and get them dead. The only thing that will put a grim smile on my ugly face when the sun comes up and I'm alive and these fuckers are stiff, rotting wood.

Maitland cried out, "Please! Please don't kill me. Please. I've got a wife and kids."

He had neither. Though he wanted kids someday. But if his view of the dark side of human nature was on the money, the wife and kids plea would be like the bells of an ice cream truck for these fuckers. He knew that it would spur them to smile and close in like the hyenas they were. Close in and get closer, closer to him, closer to judgment so they could see the lovely look of helplessness and terror on the victim's face before they snuffed him.

"Please," Maitland said.

Carl Wood started down the hill. Russell, the bald one, hesitated after a couple of steps, then stayed about twenty feet behind. Scared of the unknown down the hill, but scared of Carl too. If he turned and ran Carl may turn around and put one in his back and not really think about it; Russell knew Carl.

Carl kept coming and then Maitland could almost see his features.

Close, but not close enough and Maitland needed something to distract him, something to keep the man from raising the semi-automatic and shooting Maitland in the head.

Maitland said, "At least tell me your name." His voice regular, cold even; the panic gone.

Carl stopped, the gun at his side. It was the gun Garrett had given him. Use the nine mill, Garrett had said. Don't

119

use the shotgun. It had to be the handgun because they would use it later on the woman and then put it in the hand of the black guy, who would be dead by then.

In that moment, Carl was thinking, *my name?*

And saw the arm rise up out of the ground, a hand at the end of the arm, extending . . .

Maitland fired twice. Both shots took Carl Wood in the chest. Then Maitland shot at Russell and fired two more, but Russell was too far away. And Russell could have drawn and shot Maitland himself if he had the presence of mind to do it because Maitland only had one bullet left, but normal men don't think like that when shots are being fired on them in the dark. They panic and they run and that's what Russell did. Back up the hill as fast as he could.

Russell cleared the crest and heard the bounty hunter yell at him like a man crazed, "You better run, you piece a shit!"

Maitland reached Carl. Carl had dropped the nine millimeter. Maitland found it and put it in his pocket. Carl was groaning and coughing and gasping, the life gurgling out of him.

Carl said, ". . . how . . . ?"

Maitland said, "I've got a Kevlar vest on, dumbass."

Carl cried and seemed to laugh at the same time. Like it had to be laughed at.

He said, ". . . played me . . ."

"Right," Maitland said, feeling some satisfaction in it; feeling it though he knew he shouldn't. Alive and this man dying and it was a shameful relief bordering on joy, but there it was.

"Hey," Maitland said, "I'm gonna get you to a hospital. All right? But I want you to tell me why you tried to kill me. Tell me what you guys are up to."

". . . Shit . . . hospital . . . oh . . . oh . . ."

"What are you guys going to do to Hicks?"

". . . 'kew . . ."

Carl got it out before he died, defiant to the end.

Maitland rested on his knees for a few moments, coming down from it and trying to avoid the vomiting. The moment passed and he went through Carl's pockets, looking for identification. He found it. Carl Wood.

Maitland said aloud, "Wood?"

Then he remembered the name and said, "Oh, shit."

# SIXTEEN

Thomas Hicks had learned patience in the joint. It was not easy, but he had learned it. Learned how to work with time, not have time work against you. Time played with your emotions. Cops knew something about timing too; ask a man a question and let him sit and he'll talk rather than listen to silence. Talk himself stupid. You had to sit in the silence, deal with time. Be patient, like the Apache and the lion. Wait.

But Hicks wondered if that philosophy applied here. If they were going to take him to jail, probably it did. But if they were not taking him to jail, then what?

He had not committed any crimes since he had arrived in Kansas. He knew he had not.

So what did these local Roscoes want with him? The fame, the juice of arresting a Chicago homeboy? Something to talk about at the feed store next Monday? *Looky what we got here, boys. A Chicago nee-grow, wanted up north. He's a killer, by God. But we got his ass.* A little glory, a little excitement in a town that didn't have much. Relief from boredom.

He wished he believed that's what it was. But something was not right. If Thomas Hicks had anything, it was instinct. It had kept him alive in prison and it had kept him alive out. He knew when to leave and when to stay. If he could, he would leave now. Take his chances with the bounty hunter.

He turned around and looked at the back window. No

one there, no one following them. The other police car was not behind them. Neither was Maitland's vehicle, whatever that was.

Hicks turned back and looked out the windshield between the two cops. The assistant chief in the passenger seat, Ferguson driving.

Hicks said, "We're not going to the police station, are we?"

Garrett looked over his shoulder, like he was surprised Hicks could talk. Or think. He said, "Sure we are. We're just going to make a stop first."

Ferguson didn't say anything.

Then Wood said, "I think you're going to like what you see." He chuckled and Ferguson laughed along with him.

"Might think it's his birthday," Ferguson said.

Hicks sighed. Yeah, it was bad, whatever it was.


They turned off the county road and traveled a few miles down a dirt road. Ferguson drove on the good part of it, avoiding puddles and ruts. They reached a driveway, slowed and turned left. The drive twisted and turned into a farmer's spread. Small white clapboard house on the right, a long rectangular barn behind.

Ferguson parked the police car between the barn and the house. There were other cars there, one of them a police car with no lights on the top.

Ted Roke approached the car.

Wood and Ferguson got out, then took Hicks out of the back.

Wood said, "Everything go okay?"

"Yeah," Roke said. "How about you?"

"Fine."

"Where's Carl, Russell?"

"They'll be here soon," Wood said. "They had to take care of something."

Hicks looked at Wood because he heard something else he didn't like. Take care of what?

Wood said, "Where's Jason?"

"He's in the house."

"Doing what?"

"Staying warm, I guess."

Wood sighed.

They led Hicks into the barn. Walked to a spot on the side where a door was built into the ground, set at an angle more horizontal than vertical. Roke bent over and unlocked a padlock.

Hicks saw their intention and began to back away.

Wood said, "Larry?"

Larry Ferguson rammed the butt of his shotgun into the small of Hicks's back. Hicks stumbled and Ferguson hit him again and Hicks fell down. Roke brought out his nightstick and started to raise it.

"Hold it, hold it," Wood said. "Hicks, you're going down in that cellar no matter what. You hear me? Now you can go down there with broken bones or without. It's up to you. Now what do you say?"

Hicks kicked Ferguson in the shin.

Ferguson cried out. He was out of commission for a moment but Roke brought the nightstick down on Hicks' legs and back. Once, twice, three times.

"Larry," Wood said, "Put that shotgun down. Don't shoot him. Don't shoot him. Here get that door. Go on."

There was a lot of struggling and some more hits to Hicks and he tried to fight back but he was outnumbered and the door was opened and he was on his feet then standing on a step down, then another but he lost his balance and he fell down the rest of them. His hands were still cuffed, but they were in front of him and he managed to break his fall. Partly. It hurt like hell, though. He lay curled on the ground, groaning out his pain.

He heard the door clamp shut above him, amidst curses and someone giggling.

There was light in here.

Not much, but there was light.

Hicks, still on the ground, wondering if he had broken anything. Then he was startled by a noise, something there with him and immediately he rolled over to locate the source of noise, wondering for an instant if these sadistic rednecks had thrown him down here with a hungry animal or something. Yeeee-haw!

It wasn't an animal though.

It was a woman.

# SEVENTEEN

The woman looked at him and he looked back at her.

"Hey, Thomas! See what we're giving you?"

They heard the men laugh above them.

Wood continued, "She's all yours, boy. But if you're, you know, prejudiced against white women or something, well, you're just going to have to stay down there anyway. Larry's going to stay up here and stand guard. He's got his shotgun aimed right at the door. You got a hankering to climb up the stairs to try to get out, well, he's just gonna open up both barrels on it and shoot right through it. Understand?"

Hicks didn't say anything.

Roke said, "Ungrateful motherfucker, ain't he?"

Wood affected a frown. "No pleasing some people. Well, let's give 'em some privacy."

They giggled some more. Then Wood and Roke left.

Ferguson dragged a stool a short distance away from the cellar door. He rubbed his leg where Hicks had kicked him and wondered when they'd get to finish Hicks off.

Hicks' breathing was labored. With effort he raised himself to a sitting position, his knees and cuffed hands in front of him. He looked at the woman, about fifteen feet from him. Her back against the stone wall, her arms spread. She was not wearing handcuffs.

He said, "Who are you?"

Nina said, "Who are you?"

"I'm asking you first. Who are you?"

The woman was controlling her breathing too. Panicked.

Hicks said, "I'm not going to rape you, lady. Okay? I just want you to tell me what's going on."

"I don't know what's going on," she said, her voice edged.

"Tell me—"

"I don't know what's going on. I don't."

"Why are you here? You know that, don't you?"

"I don't know why I'm here. I was abducted. They used chloroform, I think. I woke up in here."

God, Hicks thought. She was terrified. Her face tear stained, her golden hair hanging down the sides of her face. She hadn't been beaten. But who knew what they had done to her. She was on the edge of losing it. She stood up, as if to run.

Hicks said, "Lady, I'm not going to rape you. I'm not. That's what they want me to do, but I'm not going to do it. All right? I don't rape women. That's not what I am."

Nina calmed down, a little, but she stayed on her feet.

She said, "How do I know that?"

"Well," Hicks said, "if you were listening, you might have noticed I wasn't all too eager to come down here."

". . . No. You weren't."

"Besides, I hurt too much to stand."

Hicks scooted back to the opposite wall, leaned back against it. After a few moments, Nina slid down on the ground and leaned against her wall.

She said, "They're going to kill us, aren't they?"

"They're probably going to try," Hicks said. "But I'm not so easy to kill."

Nina regarded him. A stranger, a black man. Beaten and cuffed, but not broken. His head back against the wall, his eyes closed. Even in that moment, he seemed like he *would* be hard to kill. That *he* seemed to believe it, or even affected to believe it, gave her some comfort. It was all she had.

Nina said, "What about me?"

Hicks kept his head against the wall.

"What about you?"

"Will I be easy to kill?" Her voice was firm, like she wanted to know if he was planning to leave her out of something. Telling him something then; she was not going to patronize him, but she didn't want to be patronized herself. But talking to him like he was a man, at least.

Hicks winced out a smile. Still feeling the bruises.

"I don't know, lady. I don't know about you either."

Hicks stayed where he was. His eyes shut; he didn't want to sleep. He just wanted to close his eyes for a few minutes and think about things and maybe not think, just rest and think later.

The woman spoke.

"What?"

"I said my name is Nina."

"I'm Thomas."

# EIGHTEEN

Maitland drove the Mercedes at around eighty, north on one of the county roads. Frightened, wired, cold. He gripped the wheel tight. Then there was a sign that warned him of the bend in the road and he slowed but not enough and he lost control of the car. It spun and he wrestled the wheel and hit the brakes, the car one-eightying on him and it skidded to a stop.

Maitland felt his heart race.

They can kill you, he thought. Or you can do it for them.

He put the car in gear and drove cautiously until he found a dirt road angling off. Drove down that until he reached a patch next to a couple of stone silos. Parked the car and turned off the ignition. He got out and leaned up against the car. He looked up at the constellations. Visible in this big-sky country. Pretty, but it didn't help much.

Christ. Cops trying to kill him. What do you do when it's cops that want to kill you? Not arrest you, but kill you. Tell them you used to be a cop yourself? Well, no, he had tried that. Who do you call? He had tried to use his cellular phone, but his service didn't seem to have a tower in this part of the country. Even if it had worked, dial 911 and get, what, the Union City dispatcher? So they can get a second try? Or get arrested and convicted for killing one of their reserve officers? Arrested or shot; shot, more likely.

Why? What was it the Wood brothers had against him? He didn't even know them. The bump monkey had told him that they were going to kill Hicks. Not arrest him or charge him, but kill him. For what? What had Hicks done to them? Was it a racial thing? Christ, this was the twenty-first century. Race?

Drive north and forget about it, he thought. You don't know any of these people. Drive back to Chicago, then report it. To the FBI or the state police. Not that he had much faith in the FBI; like a lot of municipal cops, he had come to regard them as the Federal Bureau of Ineptitude. The utmost combination of confidence, arrogance, and incompetence. . . . go home, then report it. *Some country cops tried to kill me. Why? I don't know. Why did I leave? Well, it was dark and they were trying to kill me. I needed to clear the area.*

Yeah, handle it that way. The smart way.

And when you get back, Charlie will understand it. Charlie will say you did the right thing.

But what about Hicks?

Will Charlie ask that question? Would it make any difference if he did not?

Well, what about Hicks. Hicks was a big boy; he could handle himself. Mead would understand that . . . why was he thinking what Charlie would think? Charlie wouldn't care one way or another. Charlie wouldn't ask Maitland to explain it. Wouldn't ask him to explain why he turned Hicks over to a bunch of cowboy cutthroats.

But they were cops. And it was in their jurisdiction. What do you want from me, Charlie?

Right. A bump monkey in a black T-shirt sitting behind the wheel of a police car. That made him a cop? Cop, my ass.

Maitland thought it then. He knew it and there was no denying it. They're going to kill Hicks. If they had the stuff to kill a white bounty hunter from Chicago they'd hesitate not at all to kill a black man wanted for murder. Maitland didn't know why and he didn't know where, but he knew their intention. And Hicks, the son of a bitch, knew he knew.

The memory came onto him then. His rookie year at Chicago PD. Standing in the break room before end of watch while the older cops argued about Jeffrey Dahmer and whether or not the Milwaukee patrol officers had fucked up. Many years ago.

After Dahmer had been arrested and charged, it came out that, a month or two earlier, two Milwaukee patrolmen had carried a sixteen year old Laotian boy back up to Dahmer's apartment after the boy had escaped. The boy had been naked. He didn't speak English, although he had repeatedly said to the officers, "No." Dahmer told the officers the boy was his lover and they had just been having an argument. The officers believed him. It was believed that shortly after the cops brought the boy back to Dahmer's apartment, Dahmer killed him. Of course at the time, the officers didn't know who or what Jeffrey Dahmer was. They just thought it was a gay thing, a lover's spat.

That day in the break room in Chicago, opinions broke about even, half supporting the cops up north, half not. Though the black and Hispanic cops tended to have less sympathy for their Milwaukee brethren than the white cops. Some said the Milwaukee cops had delivered the boy to his death, albeit unknowingly. Others said cops shouldn't second guess other cops; that they were not there and if they had been, they too would have had no idea that Dahmer was a serial killer.

Maitland, being a young rookie at the time, kept his thoughts to himself.

But he was thinking about it now. Thinking about what

his old sergeant Hector Bowen had pointed out: That the cops were white, Dahmer was white, and the Laotian boy and the women that reported the disturbance in the first place (they were black) were not. Racist or no, Hector said, they had their heads up their asses and as a result they carried a boy straight into the dwelling of a monster and the last *thought* that boy probably had was, *these cops have fucked me.*

What was it Hicks had said?

*You let them take me, I ain't gonna be alive by morning.*

And Carl Wood:

*Remember when the nigger said he'd be dead by morning? Well, he was right.*

How much more evidence do you need, homey?

Maitland said, "Dammit."

# NINETEEN

Garrett got a couple of punches in Russell's face before they pulled him off and pushed him back to the other side of the room, the chief yelling at him to calm down, Russell saying he was sorry, Garrett shouting back that he was a goddamn coward.

"Is he dead?" Garrett shouted. "You don't even know, you son of a bitch. You don't even know if he's dead or alive."

"I don't know, Garrett. It happened so fast. He probably—I don't know."

"If he's dead, you're dead. Do you hear me? If he's dead, you're dead."

"Goddammit," Bender said, "Will you calm down. Just calm down. We're not here to kill each other. Now just everybody calm down."

"He left my brother out there to die. Didn't even call us on the radio."

Russell said, "You said not to. You said not to use the radio. Chief—"

"It was an emergency, you idiot! You can use it in an emergency!"

They were in the living room of the small white house that Roke had inherited from his wife's parents. The house in front of the barn where they had the woman and Hicks locked up, their plans hitched for the time being. Three full-time police officers, one reserve, all of them sworn to uphold the law and defend the Constitution.

"All right, all right," Bender said. "Russell. What about Maitland? Is he alive?"

"He—he was when I left. But I saw Carl put two shots into him. I swear I must have seen that."

"Must have been wearing a vest," Roke said. "Was he wearing a vest when you saw him, Garrett?"

Garrett exploded. "How the fuck should I know? He had a coat on."

Bender closed his eyes. Fucking Wood brothers. Garrett should have shot the bounty hunter in the face when he had the chance. The only witness outside of them would have been Hicks and they were going to kill him anyway. But, no. He had to be clever about it, sending back his crankhead brother to do it. And Russell. Russell was all right, but he was just a reserve. A cop wannabe; the man worked at a feed store full time. Russell liked guns and he liked wearing the reserve officer uniform, but he wasn't cut out for anything serious. No one should have been surprised that he panicked and ran when he did. Russell wanted to come along; he had helped them out a good deal when he reported that the woman had asked all those questions at the diner. Russell meant well. And now Garrett wanted to kill him. How would you explain that later? Russell had family in town.

Bender said, "Garrett, Garrett. We've got to go back out there. Ted, you stay here with Larry."

Russell took them back and they found Carl near the bottom of the hill behind the shack. The bounty hunter and his car were gone. They stood around the corpse; Bender thinking, Russell shaking, Garrett breathing through his nose, controlling his rage.

Russell said, "Should we call state police, report Maitland?"

Bender said, "No. We can't do that. There's too much here."

Too much to explain. A lady from Dallas looking for her sister and a fugitive from Chicago and they would have to be killed before morning. So much to think about, to plan. Kill the woman and pin it on the fugitive. But then this goddam bounty hunter showed up and Garrett can't even kill him properly. Bad, bad planning. Garrett was not a bad officer and the men liked him, but he did not know how to administrate.

And now they had to figure Carl into it, too. Put it on the bounty hunter, maybe. But better to put it on Hicks. The fugitive from Chicago killed a reserve officer of the Union City police department, then, with nothing left to lose, went on a crime spree. Kidnapped a good-looking lady from Texas, raped her, and killed her. And then got killed himself in a standoff with the police.

Not much of a reach there. The man had already murdered two people in Chicago.

Garrett said, "I'm going to kill him."

Bender looked over to Russell, apprehensive, and Garrett saw it.

"No, not him, goddammit. Maitland. I'm going to kill him."

Hell, Bender thought.

"When?" Bender said, "When are you going to kill him? He's gone, Garrett. Probably halfway to Nebraska by now. We've got business to take care of here. Tonight. You guys started this whole damn thing; now we have to finish it tonight."

Garrett pushed back.

"You're in this too, Jason."

The men stared at each other, each of them aware the other had a gun.

Bender said, "Don't threaten me, Garrett."

"I'm not threatening you. I'm just reminding you."

Bender made a mild conciliatory gesture. "You want to kill the bounty hunter, drive up to Chicago next week and do it. But we have to take care of this woman tonight. Tonight, Garrett."

Russell said, "What about Carl? I mean, are we just going to leave him here?"

"No," Garrett said, "You already did that."

"Garrett," Bender said. To Russell, "No, we'll have to come back later and get him. We can't put him in the trunk of a patrol car. We'll have to come back later."

# TWENTY

Nina said, "It's cold in here."

Hicks said, "Pardon?"

"I said, it's cold in here."

"Yeah," Hicks said. "It's cold. We've got our coats."

"Still cold."

"Yours looks nice."

"Excuse me?"

"Your coat."

"Oh. Yeah, thank you. I got it at Nordstroms. That's a store in Dallas."

"A store, uh? That's where they sell things, right?"

"I didn't mean it like that."

Hicks said, "I know you didn't." He said, "Dallas."

"Yes. That's in Texas. That's a state."

Hicks gave a slight smile. He had no interest in making the woman feel uncomfortable. She might be all right. A good-looking white lady, but not putting on airs or anything. Or pretending she didn't notice the color of his skin, like a social worker.

Hicks said, "What are you doing here?"

"Here. You mean in Kansas?"

"Yeah."

"I came here to find my little sister. Donna. She was living here. I think she was living here. She came here with a guy. We—my mother and I—were worried about her. We were worried. So my mother asked me to drive up here and see what I could find out."

"Here?"

"Not here, this cellar. Union City."

"You said you're from Dallas?"

"Yeah. I grew up in Fort Worth."

"What would your sister be doing here?"

"God, I don't know."

"Were you tight, you and your sister?"

"Excuse me?"

"You and your sister, were you close?"

Nina regarded the man again. Who was he? A stranger sitting next to her on an airplane? A condemned man sharing a cell? A man, a human being? Putting a question to her no one else ever had. Not her mother, not Michael, no one.

"No," Nina said. "We weren't. We grew up in . . . we didn't grow up happy. We didn't have any money, no father really. And I . . . just wanted to get out."

"You look like you got money now."

Nina flushed, angry suddenly. "Well, I don't. Don't make presumptions."

Hicks raised his hands, conciliating. They were still cuffed.

"I didn't mean nothing by it."

Nina continued.

"The truth is, I don't think we even like each other very much. My mother likes her. She likes Donna, I think. But sometimes I'm not so sure. They didn't seem close when we were growing up. Or, maybe they were and I couldn't see it. Or, maybe my mother feels bad now because they weren't. And I was . . ."

"You were what?"

"A bitch, I guess. I was pretty and self-absorbed and, you know, I wanted to get out of that life. Get away.

But I didn't try to help her."

"Help who?"

"My sister. She lost her . . . she was pretty promiscuous. And I gave her a lot of shit about it, but I never asked what was wrong or if there was something she wanted to talk about. I never really offered to help her. Neither did my mom, really. But she didn't know any better. I did. I do. My sister . . . she made it hard, very hard, for anyone to like her. But she was my sister. And I left her behind."

"What do you mean, left her behind? You thought you were supposed to protect her?"

"Yeah, I think I should have. From drugs, losers, a bad, bad lifestyle."

"People do that on their own. Not much you could have done about it."

"No. No, I don't think that's true. I think we're responsible for each other."

Hicks mentally shook his head.

"Did she like you?"

"Donna? Oh, no. She hated me. She used to tell me that all the time. Kids—teenagers, they say that shit all the time. *I hate you.* But I'm fairly sure she meant it."

"Why feel bad about it, then?"

"I don't know. I think that I took a certain amount of pride in being hated by her. It meant that I was pretty, that I was successful, that I was going to go places while she wasn't. Awful. Now I realize I sold her out." Nina sighed and looked down at her clothes. Good, expensive things that looked nice on her but now were dirty and of little use to her in a barn cellar. "For this. It all seems pretty stupid now. And gross. My own sister—" Her voice cracked. "My own blood."

"Okay," Hicks said. "Okay. Take it easy now. Sometimes things happen and it ain't nobody's fault. Listen to me, lady. I don't mind you getting things off your chest, but I need to find out some things. Okay?"

"Okay."

"Now I want to ask you a few questions. Can you answer them?"

"Go ahead."

"When did you get here?"

"Here, Kansas?"

"Yes."

"Today. Jesus, today." It was hard to believe it had only been today. "I got to town and I spoke to the chief of police."

"Did he know you were coming?"

"No."

"What did you tell him?"

"I told him who my sister was. Told him I was looking for her. That I needed his help."

"Was this the chief or the assistant chief?"

"The chief."

"Did he say he knew her?"

"He told me he'd never heard of her. He told me he had no record of her being here. But later, I went to a café?"

"Cobb's?"

"Yeah, Cobb's. And this girl that works there, she had heard of my sister's boyfriend. His name was Jett Penley. Did you know him?"

"No."

"Well, this girl knew who he was. And I got excited. It was the first lead I had. So I went back to the police station to tell the chief. But when I got back there he was gone. There was this other police officer there. Roke was his name. Young, asshole cop. So I told him what I found out."

"And?"

140

"He didn't do anything. Wait, no; he told me to come back the next morning. Tomorrow morning."

"Then what happened?"

"I checked into a motel. And when I was there, the chief came over and told me he had a lead. The young cop was with him. So I got in the police car with them and the young cop put something over my face and I passed out." She said, "I woke up here. About an hour or two before you got here."

"Have they done anything to you?"

"You mean?"

"Yeah."

"No." She said, "Not yet. I don't want to think about it."

Okay, Hicks thought, she didn't want to think about it. He could understand that. But why wouldn't they? A man chloroforms a good-looking lady and throws her in a cellar in a barn, he's probably not too worried about looking like a gentleman.

And not just one man. More than one, and the chief of police behind it. Four cops out at his aunt's house, not counting the bounty hunter. They took Hicks and threw him down here with the lady and said, have at it, boy. Like he was an animal. Or he would be grateful for the opportunity, a dying man's last meal. Talk about presumptions. *Lawdy lawd, white pussy! I feel like ah's won da lottery . . .* Savages.

Not one man, but a group of men. What was it about? One man, it might be a Hannibal Lecter serial killer type of thing. Torture her before killing her, laugh while a nigger rapes her. Getting a kick.

But a group of men? And all of them cops? There had to be a reason behind it.

Hicks said, "Lady? I'm sorry to ask you this, but have

you thought about whether or not these men killed your sister?"

Nina stiffened. Her chin quivered, but she held her composure.

"Yes," she said. "I have. I guess I've been thinking that ever since I got to this town. The way Bender acted. That young cop. Creepy, this whole fucking place. There's something evil, something bloody about this town."

"I don't know if it's the town," Hicks said, "so much as it is the men in it."

"The men running it, you mean," Nina said. "They're going to kill us too, I guess. They're going to win. It's so—"

She was going to say unfair, but she stopped. But Hicks knew what she meant. Unfair, evil, an accident, an injustice.

"I know, lady," Hicks said. "I'm in it too."

"But what did you do?"

"I was here," Hicks said. "That's all." He paused. "I'm wanted in Chicago. For murder. I killed two men up there. Jumped bail and came down here. A bounty hunter from Chicago found me tonight and was about to take me back when these boys came along and took me away from him."

"What happened to the bounty hunter?"

"I don't know. He went home. Or they killed him. I see why they wanted me now."

"Why?"

"Because of you. They're going to say I killed you. They're going to put it on me. And then they're going to kill me. They use me to cancel out you, then they cancel out me." Hicks said, "That's why they wanted me to rape you."

Nina thought she was going to vomit.

"Hey, don't get sick on me," Hicks said. "I told you, I'm not . . ."

"I know, I believe you. Just give me a second." A few moments later she found her voice. "God," she said. "What are we going to do?"

Hicks said, "We'll think of something. There's only a few of them."

They remained on opposite sides of the cellar, both of them thinking to themselves. Hicks was not particularly pleased to hear what she said next, but he wasn't surprised either.

Nina said, "These men you killed. Do you want to tell me how that happened?"

Hicks looked at her. He was not angry, but he spoke plainly.

"Does it matter?" he said.

Nina Harrow was quiet for a while. Then she stood. She crossed the room and sat in the corner, at a right angle to Hicks, her back to the wall. Not next to him, but at a much closer distance, close enough that they could talk to each other in quiet voices.

"No," she said. "I guess it doesn't."

# TWENTY-ONE

The Pioneer Bar-B-Q sat off the lip of the state road as it curved around a bend, southeast to south. A gravel parking lot sloping down to the small stone-built restaurant. Vehicles parked in the lot, pick-ups mostly.

Lights beamed, round the road then flushed around as the car came into view, illuminating the dirt between the colors of the trucks. The car slowed and turned into the lot. A Mercedes 560SEC.

Maitland looked for police cars. He didn't see any so he shut off the ignition and got out. Walked inside.

The door closed behind him and he took the place in. Hearth of voices, families eating out for dinner, taking up five or six tables. They kept their caps on and drank sodas out of big red plastic cups. A heavyset woman behind the counter told Maitland he could sit wherever he liked. She looked like she was in her fifties.

Maitland looked at the menu board behind the counter.

"Just a chicken sandwich to go please," he said. "And a cup of coffee if you have any."

"Sure we got it, honey." She said, "What's your hurry?"

"Oh," Maitland said, "Just need to get home."

"Where's home?"

*Shit.*

The woman's voice was light and engaging. But the town was making him a little crazy now. He could say Chicago and maybe she'd say "Ah-hah! Get him boys!" and he'd be surrounded, bound, and taken out to the woods. The

144

thoughts of a paranoid who's losing it.

"Omaha," Maitland said.

"Really? You know, I figured you were from Nebraska."

"No kidding."

"Yeah!"

"You could tell, huh?"

"Hey, I see a lot of people in this business." She leaned forward on the counter, glad to chat. "You a cornhusker?"

"Excuse me?"

"Cornhusker fan? You know, Nebraska?"

"Oh . . . yeah. Sure."

"What do you think of their new coach?"

Maitland cocked his head and showed a frown, like he had thought about it and wanted to be fair to the man.

"You know," he said, "I think he's going to be okay."

"Yeah?"

"I really do."

"Hmmm."

"Say," Maitland said, "you got a phonebook I can use?"

"Sure."

"White pages, if you got them."

"Honey," she said, "it's all in one book."

She walked off to the kitchen to get it. Maitland shook his head at it. *What do you think of their new coach.*

She brought the phonebook back and he thanked her and quickly took it to an empty table.

He found a number and address for a C. Wood. None for Garrett Wood or G. Wood. None for Bender either. Understandable, generally. Cops don't want the populace calling them at home or driving by. But in a town like this, it was worth a shot. The woman called out to him. "You ready to roll, honey."

Maitland put a ten dollar bill on the counter. She took

it and started to get change.

"Keep it," Maitland said.

She put it in the pocket of her apron. She looked him up and down, very openly too.

She said, "You know, you're not bad looking for a husker."

Maitland smiled at her. He almost felt bad for lying, but, screw it, he'd never see her again.

"Don't tempt a lonely man," he said.

She hooted out a laugh. "Get out of here," she said.

There were no barriers where the railroad tracks crossed over the dirt road; only two small black and white signs indicating the crossing. The train clacked over the dirt road, throwing up dirt and giving some movement to a barren land. It passed and kept going west.

Maitland drove the Mercedes over the tracks at the crest of the rise then back down. Went another half mile till he saw the mailbox number he was looking for. He stopped the car, backed up and looked up at the residence.

The driveway curved up an incline to a house sitting just over a ridge, the roof visible, but the bottom of the house hidden. If there were lights on, if there were people at home, he could not tell from here. He could drive down the road and park the car somewhere, then walk back and sneak up on the place.

But it was dark now and he was tired. And the owner of this house was safely dead.

"Screw it," Maitland said, and turned the car up the driveway.

He drove up the path until the house came into view. The driveway took him behind the house. He did not see any police cars and he trembled with relief. Okay, he

146

thought, that's the upside down land you're in now; relieved not to see police cars. In back of the house were an equipment storage garage with four bays and a blue and white trailer-pull camper. There were two pickups in the garage and a strung-out Mustang. There was a light green '72 Country Squire station wagon in the grass with the tail hanging down.

Maitland shut down the Mercedes and got out. He was holding his shotgun at his side. The .38 was in his coat pocket again, reloaded now. He did a visual sweep of his surroundings and listened for sounds of people; music, television, talk. He didn't hear any. He walked to the back door of the house. It was locked. He walked around the house, looking in the windows. He did not see or hear anyone. He went back to the back door and smashed the window in with the shotgun. Reached in and unlocked the door.

There was no one home inside. There was a big screen television and a couple of thick sofas with brown felt fabric. A glass coffee table with stains on it. On the table was a bong with a Joker head on the top. There were other goblin trinkets in the house. There was a two liter bottle of Mountain Dew next to the bong, most of it finished. On top of the table and scattered around the television were several pornographic videotapes.

There was more porn in the bedroom; magazines next to the bed, a couple on top. There were guns in the bedroom too. An SKS assault rifle under the bed and three pistols in the closet. Maitland pictured Carl standing at the top of the hill, aiming the rifle down at him . . . well, it would have been bad, but it wasn't what happened. It was in the past now; Carl had chosen to use a nine millimeter handgun for some reason.

There were other bottles of Mountain Dew in the

kitchen. Not much in the refrigerator.

But a faint smell of acetone . . .

Maitland considered the signs: porn, goblins, Mountain Dew. Things he had seen before when he was a policeman.

He went back outside. No evidence that they had brought Hicks here. He stood on the back step, panned from left to right. Stopped on the camper.

Then approached it. He walked around the camper and peered into the windows. It was darker in there than it was outside, but he could tell that there was no one inside. The door on the side was unlocked and he went in. Turned on the light switch.

Maitland said, "Bingo."

It was a camper like any other. Couch built around a table. The table could be lowered and set on the same level as the couch and it would become a bed. There was another bed above the part of the camper that would hitch to the truck pulling it. The space up there had stereo equipment stuffed into it. It was the table and kitchen area that constituted the meth lab.

You could smell the chemicals as soon as you stepped inside. Acetone, toluene, ephedrine. There were pickle jars, crock pots, Coke bottles with the tops cut off. Coffee filters with bright red cherry stains on them. Nearby, the end product: yellow salt tablets, crystallized methamphetamine.

I knew it, Maitland thought. The nose knows. Carl Wood was a bump monkey and a handy little meth cook himself.

Okay then. The brother of the assistant police chief was a meth dealer. Cranked up turd taking a shot at a Chicago law enforcement officer. Nothing that much out of the ordinary, unless you're the one getting shot at. But the man was in a police car. And there had been a uniformed police officer with him. Bad enough as Friday nights go.

But then there was the brother. Garrett Wood. Assistant Chief Garrett Wood. Maitland played it back now. Garrett Wood in the dark, men around him with guns pointing at Maitland and Hicks; Garrett saying, "I don't need one" when Maitland asked him if he had a warrant. Then that other exchange when Maitland said he didn't want to see Hicks mistreated. And Wood had said, "You won't."

Right. He had been smiling when he said it. Proud of his clever retort. *You won't, Yankee boy. Because you'll be dead. Get it?* Yeah, I get it now, Maitland thought. Very funny, a laugh riot. Your brother laughed his way to the grave, you piece of shit.

Maitland could take a primal satisfaction in that. Drive back to Chicago, congratulating himself on his resourcefulness and cool head and marksmanship; discard the luck. Maybe have a good laugh himself as he put as much distance as he could between himself and the crooked cops. But he'd still be leaving a man behind. A man he was responsible for.

All right. Carl was a meth dealer and in a town this size, his brother had to know about it.

So why take Hicks? Was Hicks involved in this business? A rival meth dealer? A deal gone bad? Maybe Hicks knew about the Wood brothers, knew what they were into. And the Woods decided to kill Hicks before he had the chance to blab to straight up law enforcement. . . . yeah, that would be nice. That would make it perhaps acceptable to leave Hicks behind. Let dealers deal with dealers, as the vice squad used to say. Let the turds bury the turds.

But it didn't make much sense. Hicks was wanted for murder in Chicago. And Chicago PD would not care a fig about drug trafficking or police corruption in small town

Kansas. Like bringing buttons to an antique action. What can I get for these, sir? Er, not much, buddy.

"Shit," Maitland said.

Maitland heard a car coming.

Quickly he turned off the lights. Crouched and crept to the back window of the camper and looked out.

A Chevy Cavalier came into view and pulled in behind his Mercedes.

Maitland waited.

Whoever it was that was driving the Chevy seemed to hesitate. Mercedes . . . ? But then the driver got out. It was a girl, and she was alone. Maitland squinted and leaned forward. A young skinny girl. She hung at the back of the Mercedes, but she did not look at the license tag. She seemed to shrug it off. She walked to the back door of the house. She stopped and looked at the broken glass, and then called out something. Car? No. Carl. She said, "Carl?"

Carl did not answer back.

The girl went into the house.

Inside the camper/meth kitchen, Maitland thought about his options.

Hicks was not here. That much he knew. They were well into the night now, and Hicks had said he would be killed before the sun came up. Crazy talk, right? Well, usually it would be. But they were in Kansas now and a crank dealer driving a police car had just tried to kill a licensed bounty hunter from Chicago. A man wearing a police uniform had been with him. The crank dealer's brother—an assistant police chief—had set up the hit. So whatever Hicks was, he wasn't crazy. They were not dealing with zealous cops. They were dealing with outlaws.

Maitland walked up to the house, quietly opened the door and let himself in.

150

# TWENTY-TWO

He found her in the bedroom, rooting through a drawer of a stand next to the bed.

Maitland said, "Hey."

The girl turned around and took him in: a man in an anorak holding a shotgun at his side.

"Hey," she said. She did not seem startled. "What are you doin'?" Friendly, or trying to be. Not, what was he doing there with a gun, but more like, how're you doing? She said, "You here to see Carl?"

Maitland said, "Sort of. You seen him?"

"No," the girl said. "Not since yesterday."

"Is he a friend of yours?"

The girl shrugged. "I know him," she said.

Maitland noted the bony shoulders and hollow, sunken expression around her cheeks. Not too far gone as addicts go, but she was getting there.

Maitland said, "You here to get a tweak?" He said it in an offhand way. No judgments here, sister. Thinking, maybe it would get her to relax and open up to him.

It didn't. She shifted her feet, frowned, and looked right back at him.

"I don't know," she said. Defensive. "What are you doing here?" Meaning, what are you *doing* here, this time. "I mean, who are you?"

Maitland looked at her then, giving her a cop's stare, authoritative and business-like. Telling her she was the one in trouble here.

"My name is Maitland. I'm a bail enforcement agent from Chicago. I'm here looking for a man named Thomas Hicks. He's wanted for the murder of two men. Do you know him?"

"No. I don't know him."

"What are *you* doing here?"

The girl put her right hand on her left arm, rubbed it back and forth. Looking down.

"Answer me," Maitland said.

"I don't know. I'm just—you know . . ."

"You're here to get a bump." Maitland said, "What's your name?"

"Sadie."

"Sadie what?"

"Sadie Gravitt."

"Listen, Sadie. I don't care about what you're snorting or taking. Okay? This man I'm looking for—Hicks—I think the men that took him are going to kill him."

"So."

"Pardon me?"

"So what? You said he killed two people."

"I said he's wanted for that. He hasn't been convicted of it."

The girl shrugged again. Saying, well, that was just a formality, wasn't it. "What do you care?" she said.

"That's my business."

"Why don't you leave me the fuck alone then? Handle your business on your own."

"Don't get tough with me little girl. If you know something about the men who took Hicks and he gets killed, you'll be an accessory to murder. And that's gonna be a lot harder to deal with than a meth possession offense."

"What are you, a fed?"

Maitland didn't answer. He had told her what he was,

but if she wanted to upgrade him to a fed—or downgrade him to one—he would not stop her.

"Well?" Maitland said.

"I don't know anything about that. I don't. I'm just here to see Carl."

"Carl's dead."

The girl recoiled.

"What?"

"He's dead."

". . . how . . . ?"

"I shot him," Maitland said.

"You—"

"—he was trying to kill me."

"That's a lie."

"If you know the man, you know what he's capable of. And you know I'm not lying."

"What'd you do," she said. "Sneak up on him?"

"I don't have time to explain it to you." Maitland said, "How well do you know him?"

"I hardly—I don't know him, really."

"Well, you knew his name. And you knew him well enough to walk into his house. And you knew him well enough to accuse me of sneaking up on him." Maitland said, "What about his brother?"

"Garrett?"

Maitland smiled. "Yeah, Garrett."

"Well," the girl said, catching herself. "I mean, everyone knows Garrett. He's the assistant chief." The girl straightened up, getting her nerve back. "He's going to kill you for what you did," she said.

"Well," Maitland said, "I imagine he'll want to try. Where would Garrett be now?"

"I don't know."

"You don't know where they would have taken Hicks?"

"Hell, I don't know. To jail, I guess."

"I don't think that's what they have in mind," Maitland said. "Where else?"

"I don't know."

"Come on."

"I don't."

*"Come on."*

"Man, I don't even know this Hicks person. How would I know where they took him?"

"Okay," Maitland said, "maybe you don't know Hicks. But you know something about this, I can tell. Now stop fucking around and give me something."

"Jesus Christ, why is everyone so jumpy today? Ever since that bitch came into town everyone's been acting weird."

Maitland cocked his head.

"What bitch are you talking about?"

"Huh? Oh, I don't know. Some lady from Texas."

"Is she a fed?" Maitland said. "Is she a cop?"

"No, she's not a cop. Fucking acted like one though. Asked all these questions . . ."

"About what?"

"I don't know."

"Sadie—"

"I said I don't know."

Maitland said, "Did she ask *you* these questions?"

The girl looked at him then around so as not to look at him. Tweaker, most certainly. But not a practiced con. A bad liar.

"What did she ask you?" Maitland said. "Tell me, goddammit. What did this woman ask you?"

"She asked me about her sister. Okay. She asked about

her sister and some fucking loser her sister used to run around with."

"What about them?"

"She just wanted to know . . . where they were."

"And where are they?"

"I don't know."

Maitland gave a cop's sigh. He held the shotgun up by the stock and let the barrel slap down into the palm of his left hand. A cop's gesture of intimidation, practiced by the good and the bad . . . usually the bad.

"Sadie?" Maitland said, his voice a quiet menace. "You say I don't know once more, I may lose my temper."

The girl twisted her mouth at him. "Fuck you," she said. "You're as bad as they are. Mean, shitty . . . waving your fucking gun around. You're all the same."

"Cops, you mean?"

"Yeah, cops. You're all a bunch of fuckers."

"Right," Maitland said. "This woman from Texas, what did you tell her?"

"I told them, I didn't tell her anything."

"Excuse me?"

"I didn't tell her anything."

"You said you told them you didn't tell her anything. Who is them?"

The girl was crying now. Not sobbing, but tears rolled down her cheeks.

"Is it Garrett?" Maitland said. "Is it the chief?"

"I never spoke to them."

Oh, a little qualification there. Never spoke to them, but she sure spoke to somebody.

"Who did you speak to then?"

"I want a lawyer."

Maitland laughed.

"Sissy, I'm not arresting you."

"Well, I don't care. I'm through talking to you."

"Where is this woman now?"

"I don't—she checked into a hotel. Okay? Why don't you go fucking hassle her for a change?"

Maitland lowered the shotgun to his side. "Tell you what," he said. "Why don't we both go talk to her. Keep our stories straight."

Sadie Gravitt studied him. Quiet guy, in his way, but a fucking pig bastard like the rest. With a long mean streak in him. Goes into law so he can push people around. She said, "You kidnapping me?"

"No," Maitland said. "We're not going to call it that." He stepped back so that she could walk out of the house in front of him. "Let's go," he said.

# TWENTY-THREE

They drove back toward town in the Mercedes. The girl rode up front with him. Maitland kept the shotgun on his left, between the seat and driver's door. The girl cursed him here and there, at one point calling him a "bastard fag," a combo he had not heard before. She said, "You think you're bad, don't you. You think you're bad." And so forth and soon Maitland found himself thinking about the war on drugs.

He had been a policeman long enough to question the wisdom of the government declaring war on drugs. Did it work? Was it good policy? Did it weaken civil liberties? . . . well, like most cops, he had not been too concerned about that. Until, of course, that time a few years ago when Chicago internal affairs came after him on bogus charges and awakened the civil libertarian in him.

He had also thought about whether or not the war on drugs fostered corruption in law enforcement. Years earlier in Chicago nine cops had been convicted of extorting and/or accepting money from a mid-level Mexican cartel. Dumbasses. One of them had bought a seventy-thousand-dollar BMW and shown it off to family and friends, some of the friends being cops who were not getting a piece of the action and reported the show of wealth to their superiors. Eventually, they were all convicted. One of them said in his confession that there was just too much money there to resist. Money because the trafficking was illegal. The law against trafficking created, in itself, a market. That is, a market for police protection. Without the law, the police officers would have had nothing to sell, no leverage against the dealers. And so much goddam money there. Human nature being what it was, wasn't it just a matter of time before cops would say, I want some too?

Maitland remembered seeing a movie with Michael Keaton years ago, while he was a young officer, just starting out in narcotics. Michael Keaton played a cop that had the good fortune to be married to a woman that looked just like Rene Russo. That was hard enough to believe. While there were plenty of cops who had the everyman look of Michael Keaton, not one had a wife with the supermodel looks of Rene Russo. But then it stretched even further. In the movie, Michael Keaton stole a large chunk of money from a drug dealer that killed his partner so he could buy a house for the children of the partner the drug dealer had killed. Then Keaton killed the drug dealer, the prime witness to his corruption. Though the movie was careful to show that the killing was in self defense. Still watching? Okay. Then Keaton got caught by his lieutenant and the lieutenant (1) *let him go* and (2) *let him keep the money*.

Why? Well, because, at heart, Keaton was a "good cop."

Pure Hollywood bullshit. The movie thinking it was praising the men in blue when it was actually displaying a cynical contempt for them. And for the law they were supposed to enforce. As if to say, what can you expect from them? They're just cops.

Maitland thought then, good cops don't steal. Not from drug dealers or anyone else. He thought the same thing now.

He would admit to himself that part of his taking such offense was because he himself had killed a drug dealer. And it had been in self-defense. It was when he was working undercover. The dealer did not have it coming because he was a dealer and he needed to be taken out like yesterday's trash. He had it coming because he had already taken a shot at Maitland and Maitland had to draw and shoot or be killed.

Yeah, the "war" could be complicated. Maybe it would be easier to legalize most if not all narcotics and take away the incentives to steal, to kill, to waste untold manpower.

But then there were people like this girl. Probably not a bad kid. But look at her now in her addictive state: hollowed out, ugly, her spirit twisted. Nineteen, maybe twenty and carrying on like one of the Stygian witches. It could bring the Joe Friday out in anyone.

They got to the parking lot of the Lincoln Motel and there was not a car to be seen.

Maitland turned to the girl.

"What?" she said. "This is where she came. I can't help it if she isn't here now."

"I'm going to talk to the manager," Maitland said. "Stay here."

"Where am I going to go?"

Maitland got out. He took the shotgun and locked it in the trunk. Then he walked to the front office of the motel.

When he was out of sight, Sadie Gravitt took a cellphone out of her pocket. Dialed a number.

Russell said, "I'm busy. What do you want?"

"I'm with—"

"Huh? I can't hear you."

"I'm with this guy. Maitland. From Chicago. He said he killed Carl. Now he's looking for the woman. The woman from Texas."

"What?"

Sadie said it again. She was glad Russell was not physically with her then because he'd have probably blamed her for not speaking clearly enough and given her a slap or squeezed her arm hard enough to leave a mark.

She finished explaining it.

The next voice she heard was Garrett Wood's.

The night manager looked at Maitland's bail enforcement badge like it was foreign currency and he wasn't sure what to do with it.

Maitland said, "Did you see the woman leave?"

". . . No."

Hesitation there, and Maitland caught it.

Maitland said, "Did the police come here?"

"Uh . . ."

"Did they take her with them?"

"Now I didn't see that. I did not see that."

Maitland said, "I need to see her room."

"Uh, why?"

"She may be a witness to a murder." He left it out there and looked the man in the eye to show he was not fooling.

The night manager unlocked the door and Maitland went into the room.

There was a Coach bag on the bed. A faint smell of perfume straining against the mustiness. She had been here, but she was gone now.

Maitland said, "What time did she check in?"

"Well . . . it was during the evening news . . . I'd say between five and five-thirty."

"Thanks."

He walked back to the car, feeling better about things, but feeling worse too. Got in the car and the girl said, "I think I might know where she is."

Maitland said, "Where?"

"She smokes," Sadie said. "The closest place to get cigarettes around here is T.J.'s Corner. It's a convenience store."

Maitland regarded her.

"You thought of this just now?"

"I thought of it after we got here and we didn't see her car." The girl said, "I just want to get this over with, okay?"

"Okay," Maitland said. "How do I get there?"

"Take a right onto the road. Go about half a mile. It's just on the edge of town."

A half mile later, he pulled into the convenience store located on the corner lot. The store had a yellow and blue front, lit up and bright. A Fina station. There was a sign on the front of the lot that said there was log-home firewood for sale at old time prices. Maitland drove the car up to the front curb of the store.

He put the gear in park and turned to the girl.

"Do you know what kind of car she was driving?"

Sadie Gravitt looked back at him, her mouth open, not saying anything and Maitland felt it then; sensed trouble like a lit fuse, and then he heard the sound of a car's engine behind them and he turned around and looked out the rear window.

There was a patrol car behind him, the door opening and a young cop stepping out; then Maitland heard the passenger door of his own car open as the girl got out, then slammed it shut and Maitland didn't say "hey" or "stop" but turned back to look out the window as he saw the young cop pointing the muzzle of a shotgun right at him.

Maitland ducked and the back window exploded at the same time he heard the blast. Maitland put the gear in reverse and tromped the accelerator. The Mercedes smashed into the patrol car; Maitland held the accelerator down and pushed the patrol car out of the lot and into the street.

Roke had been the one with the shotgun. He jumped clear of his open door as the patrol car was shoved backward and he stumbled, then fell. By the time he got to his knees, the Mercedes was in the street, turning now and roaring away and Roke got one shot off, but it hit the back of the Mercedes, missing the gas tank and the tire.

Maitland had turned left and within blocks was in the center of Union City. Another police car, its light flashing and siren *whoo-whoo*-ing scared the shit out of him as it came toward him and he turned left at the next intersection, putting the car into a four wheel skid, then floored it up that road, only to see another patrol car coming toward him. He took another left, then made the next right turn into an alleyway. Which didn't work at all; he saw both patrol cars coming after him in his rear view mirror soon enough, cherries flashing angrily. He got to about sixty in the alley, shoved the gearshift into second, then made a left out into the street two blocks later.

He could see the road ahead of him rise up to a ridge where a railroad crossed over and he was afraid of blasting through any railroad crossing but there wasn't any choice because these guys meant to kill him so he hammered it and hit the crest at speed. The car got air then thumped down and he had to guide it left, *now*, because the road S-sed left then back right, but the Mercedes held onto the road through the turn, power sliding but getting back in control, and kept going.

Russell was driving the patrol car behind him, Wood riding shotgun. After clearing the railroad crossing, Russell kept the car on the road when he pushed it to the left, but he had too much momentum and when he tried to pull it back right through the second half, it was too much and the car spun into a one-eighty.

Bender was behind them in another patrol car. He knew the road and he knew Russell so he didn't slam his car into theirs, though it was close. He screeched to a halt about ten feet from contact.

Wood and Russell were out of the car, firing their side-arms down the road at the fleeing Mercedes, though it was well over a couple of hundred yards away in the dark; pumped up and wasting shots as Bender yelled at them to get in the fucking car and move it.

Maitland made a right turn, thinking it would give him more distance, and his heart sank when he saw another police car coming up behind him. This one, with its front smashed in. The young cop with the shotgun, the one that had had murder in his eyes. There was a stop sign coming up, which was not so bad, but then it was bad because a semi truck with a trailer carrying farm equipment was crossing the intersection, blocking it so Maitland hung a left a block before the intersection and drove two blocks and concrete gave way to dirt as the road narrowed and came to a dead end at a steel gate.

# TWENTY-FOUR

Hicks said, "Listen." He raised his head to the ceiling.

"What?" Nina said.

"Do you hear anything?"

Nina waited and listened. She said, "No."

"If you listen," Hicks said, "you hear someone. Moving around, clearing his throat. But that's all."

"Yes?"

"What I'm saying is, there were two of them earlier. Talking. Now there's just one. The other one left."

Nina said, "Maybe he went to the toilet."

"No. His radio squawked. He spoke into it . . . and he left."

"Where, though? And for how long?"

"I don't know."

"Thomas, there was one man here when they put you down here."

"Yeah, but maybe he's asleep. Do you know what time it is?"

"No. You?"

"No. But I know it's late."

They both sensed it was late. Late enough to feel tired, enough to feel your head thrumming with fatigue. But they were too frightened to sleep.

Hicks said, "Maybe he's tired. Maybe he's got no one to talk to, no one to watch him and tell him to pay attention to us."

"And if he's not?"

"Maybe he is."

Nina shook her head.

"There's a padlock on that door. What are you going to do, push it open with your head?"

"I don't know," Hicks said. He felt defensive and foolish. Goddamn woman talking more sense than him. He felt like a fresh convict, looking at the confines of his cell, deluding himself into believing he was the first one to think of how to bust out. But that was doing time in a cell, not waiting on death row hoping for a reprieve from the governor before the sun came up and they fired up the zap seat. He said, "We can't just sit here."

Nina said, "You go up those steps and hit that door, that cracker will blow your head off."

Hicks studied her for a moment. Then he laughed.

"Cracker?" he said. "What, are you trying to sound like a sister?"

"Sound like a—what, because I said 'cracker'?"

"Yeah."

"Well, believe it or not, black people aren't the only ones that use that word. That's what I was called, growing up."

Hicks was still smiling.

"Really?"

"Yes, really."

"Huh. But they don't call you that no more, do they?"

"They certainly fucking don't," she said. With authority.

Hicks wondered about her. Not just about who she was and how she got here, but about her. What she liked, how she lived. He wondered if it would help to talk about personal things: husband, children . . . maybe it would help them calm down, rest, not think about dying. But then he remembered that they had thrown him down here to rape her, to help them build up whatever fucked up thing they were going to do. He thought that if he said something personal to her now, it might spook her. *What you got in mind, boy?* White women could be like that, when a black man got personal. Not that he knew from experience, but he had witnessed it standing on the sidelines and sometimes it upset him even though he wasn't in it. It was a thing he avoided discussing with black women; a thing he avoided discussing in general. Some of the women in his past could get downright evil if they saw a brother with a white lady. And these were not all angry women either. Hicks would not even joke about it around them. Though he would smile when his friend William imitated the sisters in their fury. *Rich nigger wants two things: Lexus and a white woman on his arm.*

Nina said, "What are you smiling at?"

"Nothing."

"I'm amazed you can smile at something like this," she said. "Don't you get scared?"

"Sure."

"You have a family?"

"No."

"No wife?"

"No."

"Ever been married?"

"No."

Nina waited, but Hicks didn't say anything else.

Nina said, "I'm engaged."

"Hmmm. When are you getting married?"

"I don't know." She sounded fatigued when she said it.

"You'll see him again," Hicks said.

Now Nina smiled. He didn't understand. Didn't understand that she was unsure about all of it now. Unsure of Michael, unsure of the path she had charted out for herself. You can plan it out all so carefully and then in the space of a day it gets derailed and then you're not even sure you want to put it back on track.

Nina moved closer to him. She lowered her voice and said, "You said earlier there's not many of them, right?"

"Yeah."

"I think we have a chance if we wait . . . until morning. Wait until they get close to us. Then we try something."

"Like?"

"I don't know. Like getting one of their guns away from them and using it. You've used a gun before, haven't you?"

'Cause I'm black? Hicks thought. . . . well, he had told her he killed two men.

"Yeah, I have."

"Good," she said and meant it. "Can you wait?"

Hicks looked at her again. Rich white lady asking him, an ex-con, could he wait? And then getting him to confirm that he knew how to kill a man. Yeah, I have killed. And she says, *good*. Hmmm.

Lady's fiancé better watch this one.

# TWENTY-FIVE

It was a four post fence and Maitland stepped on the second rung then swung himself up and over and ran half the length of a football field before Roke screeched his patrol car to a stop and by the time Roke got out Maitland had another twenty yards on him, fading into the darkness and then into a grove of cedar trees. Roke stuck his shotgun out that way and fired it, pumped and fired it again, but it was useless at this distance; good for shooting rabbits coming out of a hole twenty feet away but not much good beyond thirty yards in darkness.

Maitland heard the shots and stopped in his place in the trees, thinking, he can't see you, he hasn't got the spotlight on, he can't see you so stop running or you'll run into the path of his shot, stop running and think.

Beyond the grove he saw a white grain elevator, about eleven stories high, and a church beyond that. He thought briefly, like a drunk, if the church would offer him sanctuary then smiled at the notion, thinking, you're not in Spain or Mexico, fool; in a place like this, the deacon is likely to be a reserve officer.

But the young cop in the patrol car, the one with the shotgun, he had to have seen Maitland run into the grove. Maybe he did, maybe he didn't . . . maybe he got there too late to see where Maitland had run. Maybe the young cop had poor night vision. . . . Shit . . . Well, he could stay here and hope the cop had not seen him run in, pray for it, and reach Amen as the young cop came crashing through the brush, yelling *"Yee-hah"* or "I got him boys," before blasting him to pieces. He could wait for that or he could keep moving.

Roke stood on the side of the fence nearer the cars and looked out into the darkness. He could not see the bounty hunter. He flashed his spotlight out on the field and the grove—after he fired the two shots—but he saw nothing. They needed more men. They needed a helicopter from State Police to fly over the damn place and light it up like a bar at closing time. But they were not going to get that because Jason and Garrett said they would have to handle this thing themselves.

Roke could understand that; not wanting state police involved or county sheriffs either. They were up to some dirty shit and if outside agencies got involved they might take the bounty hunter alive and the bounty hunter would tell them about Carl and then Sadie Gravitt and the bitch from Texas . . . and then what? Garrett would say some bullshit like, "I'll take care of it, don't worry." And then KBI or FBI or some state fuckers would separate them all and start asking them the same questions and get different answers and they would all be fucked. And they couldn't have that shit, so the bounty hunter needed to die.

But as Ted Roke stared into the darkness on the side of the fence he thought was safe, he thought of Carl Wood, dead now with a couple of the bounty hunter's bullets in him. He thought of that and he hesitated.

He felt lights on his back and turned to see a patrol car roar up behind him. Then another one. The chief, Russell, and Garrett got out of the cars and were standing next to him.

Roke, making his voice sound firm, said, "He's out

there." Like he'd done something positive.

It didn't work. Garrett said, "Yeah? What are *you* doing?"

Roke pretended not to catch his meaning.

"I was waiting."

"For it to start snowing?" Garrett said.

Bender didn't have time for this. He said, "Garrett, take Russell with you in the patrol car, circle back to Willson Street and see if you can find him. Ted and I will walk through the field. Go."

Minutes later, Russell turned the patrol car right onto Willson Street and drove toward Immaculate Heart, the red brick church built before the Great War. The grain elevator towered behind it, two impressive structures framed against the clear blue night. They slowed as they got to the church and turned the spotlight on the church and the parking lot next to it. Drove around the church and lit up the parking lot and the flat fields to the west.

From the east, Bender and Roke came through the small field and then, cautiously into the grove of cedar trees, Bender shining his flashlight while Roke held his shotgun with both hands. They picked their way through the trees then came out to more field and the church parking lot on the other side. After a few moments, Russell and Garrett pulled up next to them in the patrol car.

Wood said, "No sign."

"All right," Bender said. "We're going to look under every car here. Garrett, you and Russell check the church. Careful. He's armed."

Garrett said, "I know that." Then moved off.

Bender said, "Ted, you start on that end, I'll start here. He's around here somewhere."

The men complied with his orders, even Garrett. He walked

off with Russell, Russell saying, "God*damn* cold out here."

They searched for almost forty minutes. It wore on them. Garrett got even more irritable, Russell more apprehensive, Roke gripping his shotgun too much. Bender kept his cool, though he was conscious that the night was passing and they had business to take care of.

He called his men in and they stood in the church parking lot talking.

Roke pointed west and said, "He must have gotten across those fields."

"No thanks to you, dumbshit," Garrett said.

Russell said, not thinking, "No, I checked those fields. I didn't see anything."

Garrett said, "You shined a light on it, that's all." He got back on Roke again. "Maybe he circled back to his car. Maybe he's in town now, smoking a cigarette."

Roke held the stock of his shotgun against his hip, between being scared and being pissed. He said, "I think I'd've seen him if he tried that."

Bender said, "Christ," directing it to both of them, the punks. "All right. We're just going to have to deal with him later."

Garrett said, "Later?"

"Yes, later, goddammit." Bender turned to Roke. "What about your vehicle?"

Roke said, "I think the radiator's busted."

They were about twelve blocks from the station.

Bender said, "Get it back to the station, switch it out with Unit Fourteen." Unit Fourteen was an '88 Caprice, an embarrassment. Bender said, "Ted? Don't stop and bullshit with the dispatcher. Switch cars and get back out to the house, ASAP. Clear?"

"Yes, sir."

The four of them rode back to where they had left the two patrol vehicles on the other side of the field. Roke was filled with relief when he saw that Maitland's Mercedes was still there, though he succeeded in not showing it. They got out and looked it over just in case the man was hiding inside. He wasn't.

Then Garrett gestured to the car and said, "What about this?"

Bender opened the passenger door. He saw a cellular phone on the console. He picked it up and put it in his pocket.

Roke said, "Should we impound it?"

Bender imagined a phone call to Lew Tait, the man the police contracted towing services with. Lew asking, "Whaddaya got, chief?" as he hoisted the back end of the Mercedes up with its Illinois tags.

"No," Bender said. "Take the tags off and put 'em in my unit."

Russell took off the tags with the screwdriver of his Swiss Army knife. Before he was finished, Bender sensed what the men wanted, could feel the destruction in the air. Sure enough, when Russell put the tags in the chief's car, Roke said, "He can still drive the car, though. If we leave it here, and he comes back, he'll be able to use it."

"Right," Bender said. "Well, go ahead and disable it."

Roke circled around to the side of the hood, pointed it down at an angle and blasted a hole through the driver's side front tire. He walked around to the front of the car, pumped a shell and blew another round into the windshield, exploding it. Russell and Garrett laughing now. They drew their weapons and joined in, blasting out every window the car had. Soon the tires were all gone and there were holes plunked through the doors and hood, ruining the cylinder head. The car sagged as if it had died and they stopped.

Well, Bender thought, they needed to take some of the steam off.

He said, "Let's go."

The wind gusted again and Maitland winced as it went right through him. He crossed his arms and held himself. God, it was cold. Chicago cold, except he was not standing on a corner waiting for the warmth of a cab or even a bus. He was on the top of a grain elevator, lying on his back and staring up into the sky, wondering if the wind would freeze him like hard cookie dough before rolling him off the side to plunge to his death.

When he heard them start the patrol car, he decided that the smart thing to do was stay up here for a while. Maybe they left a man in the parking lot and if Maitland tried to climb down the ladder and they spotted him, he'd be toast. Especially if they were smart enough to let him climb about halfway down. *There he is!* Then laying up a volley of shots which he would have to just wait for because there wouldn't be time to scramble back up the ladder and he couldn't very well keep climbing down. They would shoot him then watch him fall and later they would wonder if the shots or the fall had killed him. So he stayed where he was.

A few minutes later he heard the gunfire. His heart thudded and it took him a moment of panic to realize they weren't shooting at him. Distant gunfire. But not too distant. It continued and he thought, what? What are they doing? He moved to the side of the roof and looked over the eastern side to see muzzle flashes beyond the trees. It took him a second to discern that they were not shooting each other. They were shooting at his car, killing it.

Maitland, jaw slightly ajar, watched his ride home taken apart, then destroyed.

They were about four hundred yards away. . . . Maybe with a high powered rifle and a night vision scope he could end it right here. Then he thought, shit, what good would that do? He had never been a tact team guy; SWAT had never appealed to him. Bunch of guys itching to kill someone and resenting the mediators that tried to talk the turd inside the house out of murdering his family or the hostages in the convenience store. More often it was family . . . Anyway, all he had now was a five shot Smith and Wesson snubnose. A great gun, but strictly for close combat. A spy's gun, not a soldier's. Five shots, which he had planned to use on the first five assholes who tried to come up that ladder. But that did not seem likely now; they were blasting his car because they couldn't find him and they were pissed off and someone or something was going to take a beating.

So, yeah, that was a good thing.

But mercy, it was cold up here. Dangerous cold. Too cold to stay up here all night. He had left his gloves in the car, along with his shotgun and, shit, his cell phone. He had the anorak on and a decent sweater underneath. But that was metropolitan clothing; Saturday at the antique shop clothing; drive from Chicago to Kansas clothing; it was not fit for climbing mountains, which he might just as well be on now. If he stayed up here all night, he might survive. He could punch himself awake, fight off sleep so he wouldn't freeze to death. Climb down in the morning . . .

He remembered getting a call when he was a young patrolman. Dispatch telling him and his senior partner that a lady on the Gold Coast of Lakeshore Drive saw a man in her yard which was on Lake Michigan. They got there and found the guy passed out on the grass. It was late September, about two o'clock in the morning. The guy was wearing shorts and a T-shirt; shivering in a way that was frightening. The guy managed to talk; said he had been wind surfing.

Maitland's partner, Johnny Shrum, figured it out.

"Jesus Christ!" Johnny said. "This is the guy they've been looking for!"

Earlier on the ten o'clock news, there had been camera crews lakeside reporting a breaking story. Two guys went wind sailing after they got off work. A storm came up, unexpected and violent. The skies darkened and the temperature dropped thirty degrees. The winds picked up to speeds of forty miles per hour. The water on Lake Michigan got too rough and they had to call the rescue helicopters and boats in. They only saved one guy. The other one was still out there; they couldn't find him.

Every reasonable person presumed the second man would be dead by morning. The only thing left to do was to wait for his body to wash ashore.

But the second man was one of those tri-athelete freaks that could swim for miles and had that stubborn human instinct to keep living. The guy managed to do it, even though he didn't have a wet suit. He swam more than two miles and ended up about three miles from where he started. He survived. He had been in the water from five in the evening till two in the morning. He lost his surfboard around seven.

Maitland and Shrum brought the man in the woman's house and wrapped him in blankets while they waited for the paramedics to show up with a special unit that had an oven-like device to prevent death by hypothermia. The guy spoke to them because he needed to speak and he told them his story.

He said that he could not remember everything, but he remembered getting to an inlet after several hours and climbing into a small rowboat anchored in the middle of the harbor. Then lying on his back in the boat, looking up at the sky himself. But it was still cold outside, around fifty degrees with the wind blowing and he was soaked and he realized that he did not have the strength to unmoor the boat and he sensed that if he stayed where he was he would almost certainly die. And then he realized that he . . . would . . . have to climb back in the water and keep swimming.

Which he did. Swam another couple of hundred yards, came out of the water and passed out in the lady's yard. The guy said he knew it was dumb, but he thought that climbing back into the water was the worst part.

Maitland thought about it now.

He thought, well, that guy probably felt worse than I do.

Then thought, but it was cold water he had to deal with. Not men with guns.

He watched the patrol cars leave. He waited another twenty minutes before he climbed back down.

# TWENTY-SIX

Maitland looked at the Mercedes from a distance. Watched it for fifteen minutes before deciding there was no one there waiting for him. Then he walked up to it.

All the windows were shot out, all the tires exploded. Holes all over the sides like a bad skin condition. Maitland told himself it was just a car. It was not like losing a lung.

But he felt worse when he looked inside and found that they had taken his cell phone. And again he thought about how far he was from civilization. No phone. He tried to open the trunk of the car to get his shotgun, but the impact of the crash with the police car earlier had jammed it shut. The only good thing he got were his gloves, which had been in the console where he left them.

He walked away from the car, got off the roads and through yards and abandoned lots. He walked back towards the center of the town. He was aware of this, but there was no getting away from it. There was nothing for him outside of town except cold fields and exposure to the elements. He needed a car.

The main street of Union City was quiet and empty, asleep for the night. The town's lone red light flashing for traffic that wasn't there. Maitland looked down the street. Empty spaces, two-story buildings that may have been small department stores thirty years ago, but now only the bottom floor was used; an antique shop; second-hand clothing. Signs of commerce and life, but closed down for now. He kept looking and three blocks ahead he saw colored plastic triangles dangling from a rope. A used car lot.

Maitland had learned how to hot wire cars when he worked undercover in narcotics. Not so he could steal cars, but so he could fit in with the element. That was mostly what undercover work was, fitting in. Acting, but you kept certain things you learned for the role.

There were about a dozen vehicles on the lot. An even assortment of cars and pickups, the most expensive one worth about twelve grand. Maitland stopped at a brown 1970 Chevy Malibu. Plain with stock rims. For now he liked plain and nondescript. He remembered a Richard Pryor line about stealing cars. Something to the effect of, "Chevy, man, that's a jack-off. Now a Jaguar, that's pure pussy." On a night like this, Maitland would opt for the jack-off.

The Chevy was locked so Maitland went back to the alley and found a coat hanger between a dumpster and a discarded washing machine. He brought the hanger back, twisted it, and slid it over the top of the window to loop it around the door lock and he heard the car coming, which was not good, but then it got worse because before he turned he heard the engine roar, accelerating and high beams were on him and there was a police car, another one, bearing right down on him.

The car screeched to a halt about ten to twelve yards in front of him and Maitland saw that it was the young cop, getting out of the car now, the door opening and creating a space between it and the car and the young cop would be in that space only a moment because he would have to stand up to point that shotgun at him and there would only be that moment, it would not come again, and the cop stepped out into the space and Maitland shot him.

The shot punched Roke between his chest and shoulder and he flailed back and dropped the shotgun and then he was lying on the ground. Then the bounty hunter was next to him, taking the shotgun and throwing it into the street. He took Roke's sidearm too. It was a .357 revolver. Maitland put it in his pocket.

Roke gasped in pain and disbelief. "You shot me, you piece of shit. You shot me."

Maitland said, "I got tired of running."

Roke gasped again.

"You're a dead man."

"Right," Maitland said. He sighed. Christ, this guy was going to bleed out and then *he'd* be the dead man.

Maitland checked his pockets for a handkerchief. He didn't have one. So he took his gloves off and pressed them against the man's wound. Roke winced.

"Christ. Don't torture me. Don't—"

"I'm not torturing you, you idiot. Here, hold that against the wound. Firm. Just hold it there." He said, "Where's the nearest hospital?"

The young cop looked at him curiously. And Maitland asked him again.

"Where is it, boy?"

Roke said, "Down this street. About two miles."

Maitland helped the man up and put him in the front of the police car. Roke slumped against the window, his head resting there, but he was breathing. Maitland got the car moving. Then he heard the man weeping.

"Calm down," Maitland said. "You're not going to die. What blood type are you?"

"Oh. O-positive. Are you asking me in case I pass out?"

"Yeah."

"You'll get yours, too, man. You'll get yours."

Maitland thought, fucking ingrate. Mean *and* stupid. He looked over at the young cop and shook his head. He said,

"Just what are you fucking clowns up to?"

"Piss off."

"Hey," Maitland said, "keep up that kind of talk and I'll dump your ass out on the side of the road. You'll bleed out in about thirty minutes."

"I'm not telling you anything. You're the enemy."

"And those guys are your friends?" Maitland said, "Tell me something, were you trying to kill me 'cause you thought it'd be fun, or was it because your chief wants to kill Hicks and the woman from Texas and I know about it?"

Roke smiled. "Both," he said, before passing out.

He laid on the horn of the police car as he pulled up to the doors of the emergency room. Helped the ER doc get Roke out of the car, then Roke was in the doctor's arms and a nurse was helping him get Roke on a stretcher. Maitland said, "His blood type is O-positive. You got that? O-positive." And then he was back in the police car and gone.

A couple of minutes later, the scrub nurse said, "Is that guy coming back?"

Garrett and Bender rode together in the chief's car; Russell followed behind, driving tandem out to the house where they were holding the captives.

They were quiet for most of the drive, Garrett behind the wheel, his eyes on the road, Bender sitting and thinking. But he could not pretend to be unconcerned for long and eventually he spoke.

"Earlier tonight, when you picked up Hicks," he said. "What did you say to the guy?"

Wood said, "What did I say to Hicks?"

"No. What did you say to the bounty hunter?"

"I told him we were taking Hicks, whether he liked it or not."

"That all?"

"I think so. Why?"

"What I'm asking is, did you say something personal to the man?"

"If I did, I'd tell you." Wood said, "What difference does it make?"

"I'm just wondering what he's still doing here. Wondering why he would go to the hotel and ask about the woman, why he would care about what happens to a black guy wanted for murder."

Wood said, "He's a bounty hunter. He doesn't bring back Hicks, he doesn't get paid. That's why it's good that we destroyed his vehicle. Let him know that being here isn't profitable."

"Okay," Bender said. "But how's he going to leave town without his vehicle?"

Wood said, "I don't want him to leave. He's going to die here."

Bender thought, so are you, Garrett. So am I. Though Garrett had never really tried to leave Union City. Jason Bender had. Twice he had tried to leave. Once when he applied for the state highway patrol. It would have been a significant boost in pay and prestige. It would have meant moving to Topeka or Wichita or KCK or someplace better, but they turned down his application and told him he could try again in two years. He didn't. The second time he tried to leave Union City, he set his sights lower: Hutchinson PD. He heard there were openings and called a captain that was conducting the interviews to schedule an appointment. The telephone call went badly. The Hutchinson captain spoke to Bender like he was a child, said things like "I just told you what you need to bring. Did you not understand me?" At the time, Bender was assistant chief at Union City. No one had spoken to him like that since he was a kid and his face reddened and he thought briefly about driving up to Hutchinson just to kill the man. But he didn't. He never showed up for the interview at all. It was about a year after that that the previous chief got drunk and killed the two kids, opening up the chief's spot for Bender. In charge now at Union City, though his salary was still less than that of a State Trooper. The radio squawked. And then there was a voice, vaguely familiar.

"This is Unit Fourteen, calling Chief Bender. Unit Fourteen calling Chief Bender."

Bender looked over at Wood. Unit 14 was the old Caprice Bender had told Roke to commandeer. But it was not Roke's voice they were hearing on the radio.

"This is Unit Fourteen. Jason, what's your twenty?" The man said, "Where are you?" A voice that said, I'm looking for you. No, not Roke.

Bender picked up the handle.

He said, "What are you doing?"

Maitland said, "I'm trying to get out of town."

Bender said, "Go then."

"I would, but my car needs repairs. And there's no mechanic working at this time of night. Not in a town like this."

Bender said, "It's a nice town."

"Right," Maitland said. "Good place to raise a family. Say, can you send out, uh, one of your 'officers' to have a look at the damage to my car? I think it may have been local gangsters. Small towns have them too."

"Well, to tell you the truth, I'm a little short handed tonight." Bender said, "You say you're in Unit 14, Roke with you?"

"No. He's in the hospital. Gunshot wound."

Garrett and Bender exchanged looks.

Bender said, "Is he alive?"

Maitland, the ex-cop, knew bogus compassion when he heard it. Especially when it came from brass. Maitland said, "Do you care?"

Bender said, "He's one of my men."

Maitland said, "And what have you and Wood gotten him into, Jason?"

"That's police business," Bender said.

Maitland said, "Sending crank dealers out to kill people is not police business. What are you up to, Jason?"

"Hey, Maitland?" Wood took the handle. "This is Assistant Chief Wood. You want to ask questions, motherfucker, why don't we meet someplace and I'll give you an answer."

Maitland remembered the man. Smiling when he said, "You won't", giving him what he believed would be the sign off. Maitland said, "Yeah, Garrett? Who you gonna send this time?"

"I'm coming this time. You're not gonna get the jump on me like you did Carl, you piece a shit. You hear that? I'm coming this time."

Maitland said, "Tell me where you've got Hicks and the woman, and maybe I'll meet you there."

Bender said, "I don't know what you're talking about."

Maitland said, "You've got Hicks. And Roke told me you took the woman." Maitland pursed his lips, a man waiting for the next card at the blackjack table, hoping he doesn't bust.

After a moment, Bender said, "How much did he tell you?"

"He told me you've got the woman. He told me she's from Texas. He told me everyone's been jumpy since she got into town."

Wood said, "I think you're talking out of your ass. I don't think Ted told you anything."

"Maybe so," Maitland said. "But you can't be sure, can you? Over." Maitland clicked off and put the handle back.

Bender said, "That guy's a cop. Or he used to be."

Wood said, "You don't know that."

"I know. Civilians don't talk like that. They don't call cops gangsters."

"I didn't hear him say that."

Bender said, "You weren't listening." He wasn't going to explain it.

Garrett Wood thought, the guy is a dead man, whatever he is. He had killed Carl and he was going to die. But calling the chief by his first name . . . ? It was something a cop would do. Familiar, yet pointed. It was the way cops talked to gangsters.

Bender said, "Pull over."

Garrett slowed and pulled onto the side of the road, careful to keep all four wheels from sliding off into the ditch. Russell pulled over behind them.

Garrett turned to him.

"Well?"

"Let me think for a minute," Bender said.

After a few moments, Garrett said, "I thought you wanted to go back out to the house, finish it."

"I know what I said. Just let me think for a minute."

Christ, Garrett thought. Jason was letting this Chicago cop get to him. But it could be good. Maybe Bender would change his mind, they'd go back and find the man and put him down.

They went back to town, after all. After what happened, they didn't have much choice.

# TWENTY-SEVEN

On a back street in town, Maitland stopped the car and looked in the back. He had thrown the young cop's shotgun back there earlier and he remembered seeing something. A jacket. The young cop's blue coat. It was a nice one, shiny and well kept. Maitland got out of the car and opened the back door and picked up the coat. He found a checkbook in the inside pocket. Ted Roke's name and address were written on the checks.

For a moment, he thought about writing a check to himself. Pay to the order of Evan Maitland—replacement vehicle. Piece of shit.

He looked at where he was. Standing next to a police car that they would know on sight. Come up on him and pump the thing full of buckshot. He needed another car. He also needed to draw Bender and Wood back to town and away from Hicks. Maybe Hicks and the woman, if the woman was still in this godforsaken place.

He thought, but then where will you go?

Maitland remembered then that he was close to the used car lot where he had almost stolen the '70 Chevy Malibu. The jack-off Chevy. Before Roke got there, had he got it unlocked?

It turned out that he had. He got inside the Malibu, found the wires he needed to find and bound them together. The Malibu's 350 engine kicked into life.

Maitland moved quickly then, conscious of the fact that he was right out on Main Street, the red traffic light

185

flashing. He took the policeman's shotgun and coat out of the patrol unit and put it in the Malibu. He tore open the inner lining of the jacket and got a piece of fabric long enough to make a tourniquet. He twisted it like a cord and shoved it halfway into the gas tank receptacle of the patrol unit. Then he set the cloth aflame with a cigarette lighter.

He ran to the Malibu, put it in gear and shot out into the street. The tires squealed as he made a hard left and accelerated away from the police car. He got about eighty yards down the main street when the back of the police car exploded. He saw orange flame plume up and dance against the dark. And he smiled. *You destroy one of mine, I'll destroy one of yours.* If Bianca were here, she'd tell him that he was disgusting. Juvenile and base. . . . Okay, so he was. But goddamn, it felt good.

# TWENTY-EIGHT

The police dispatcher on duty at the police station heard the explosion as well as anyone else in town. But within minutes the 911 calls poured in, all reporting the same thing. She dispatched the call to the fire station and all available police units. It was not possible for Chief Bender and Garrett Wood to ignore the call—a car had been blown up right on Main Street. A police car. Bender and Wood turned the unit around and drove back into town.

Within minutes they were standing on a street watching the skeleton of Unit 14 burn against the night. Both of the town's fire trucks were at the scene; Barney, the fire chief, directing the town's one fulltime firefighter and about six volunteer firefighters, in civilian pants and coats, holding hoses and looking scared and confused. This was not a barn burning.

Fire chief Barney Withers sought out Jason Bender.

"We don't see anyone inside the car!" He shouted over the chaos, though Bender did not think it necessary to do so. "I'm danged if I know how it happened!"

Bender said, "Probably just kids."

"Kids?" Barney Withers said, "Kids blowing up a dang police car? For heaven's sake, kids don't do this!"

Barney was a deacon at the local Nazarene church. He was about fifteen years older than Chief Bender. Bender had never heard him swear. That he would say dang was enough to demonstrate that he was angry and frightened.

Bender said, "It's not that big a deal. It's not one of our regular units."

187

"It's city property, Jason."

Bender was starting to get on edge. People seeing him here at this hour . . . they'd be able to place him later. *I saw Jason at two in the morning. In uniform too. What do you think of that?* Barney raising his voice, leaning on him. Kids don't do this. Old fool. Bender regretted not having forced Barney out before this. But Barney had not gotten along with the old chief; he had thought the old chief was an immoral man, an unregenerate drunk. And Barney had been right about that. But now Barney was making a big thing out of a blown up police car, like it was the sign of some godawful insurrection.

Bender said, "I'll take care of it, Barney. Okay? Go on."

Barney walked off, but not before giving Chief Bender a look that had some challenge in it. Old bastard. Bender looked at the ruins of the police car. They had gotten the fire out now and there was more smoke drifting over the street; heat still radiated out into the cold night air. The firefighters kept the water on it still at the direction of the fulltime fire captain.

Bender looked at it and thought, it's unreal. Christ, maybe it is an insurrection. A man blowing up a police car. This after putting a policeman in the hospital. A man challenging police authority itself. That's an insurgent, right?

But then the man had appeared in his office this very day in clean clothes with proper documentation and had asked him to comply with lawful process. It was the same guy. The same guy who wouldn't call Jason Bender "chief" anymore. Just called him by his name. It was a psych tactic that every police detective used to take away power from the suspect. Belittle him, let him know he's only worth as much as his first name. And that was what this goddamn bounty hunter was up to. Belittling Jason Bender, yes, but telling him something else too. Telling Bender he didn't really consider him a cop anymore.

Wood walked up. He said, "I think he's out of here now. This was the last thing he did before he left. Like a drunk throwing a brick through a bar window after he's been thrown out."

Bender sighed. "No," he said. "He's around here some-where."

"I should have killed him myself," Wood said. "This evening, when I first saw him, I should have killed him then."

"Yeah," Bender said, "but you didn't."

Ted Roke's house was not far from the town's main street. It was on a residential block, houses on both sides. The houses looked like they had been built in the twenties. It made Maitland nervous to be this close, but there was nothing else that could be done. He found the house number but parked in the alley behind it.

He left the shotgun in the car, but he took the .38 with him. Walked through the backyard and up to the backdoor. It was unlocked. Maitland went in.

He was in the kitchen. He let his eyes adjust to the dark-ness. Shapes and objects began to take form: a small white Formica table, a refrigerator with a broken handle. He heard the sirens coming from the front of the house.

The front door was open.

Slowly, he walked out of the kitchen, through the dining room, then the living room. The sirens getting louder now, then winding down as they found the fire. He could feel the cold air coming through the front door. He put his hand in his pocket, rested it on the .38, as he edged toward the door.

Through the doorway he saw a woman standing on the

porch. Slim and dark haired, wearing a heavy blue bathrobe and slippers. She was smoking a cigarette, looking out to the front.

Maitland stepped out on the porch.

"Hey," he said.

She turned, startled, and stepped back away from him.

She was olive skinned, and her nose was big. Attractive, in an unconventional way. Hispanic perhaps, or Arabic. Her curves set well against the fabric of the robe.

She said, "Who are you?"

"I'm not here to hurt you," Maitland said.

"Who are you?"

"My name's Evan."

"What are you doing in my house, Evan?"

"I'm sorry. It was necessary." He said, "Are you Officer Roke's wife?"

"Yes."

"Did you know that he's been shot?"

Mrs. Roke dragged on her cigarette, her other arm tucked around her waist. She exhaled.

"Yeah, I know."

There was something off about the way she said that, Maitland thought. Nonchalant. Maybe to show she was a tough frontier wife. Maybe . . .

Maitland said, "You know?"

"Yes." She shrugged. "The hospital called me."

"Well—what are you doing here?"

"They said he's going to be fine. He'll be there for a couple of days."

Maitland waited. He was fairly sure he understood it now. But he spoke anyway.

"You don't want to visit—"

"No." She looked directly at him, her eyes frank and unashamed. Maitland thought, well, Officer Roke seems to have made an honest woman of her. She kept looking at him.

Maitland said, "Will you be here when he gets out?"

"I don't know. Are you offering to take me away?"

Maitland shook his head. He said, "Does he mistreat you?"

"Yes."

She was not going to say anything else. It was dark on the porch. You could not see any bruises on her face or neck. But a practiced abuser knows where to hit so that bruises don't show, even in good light. And there are abuses beyond physical violence: trying to pimp her to friends, calling her a whore, etc. She was not going to give specifics and he was not going to ask.

The sirens were off now. They could hear the faint sound of the fire engines idling, men shouting, horns, water nozzles.

The woman said, "You're not from here."

"No."

"What are you doing in a place like this?"

"I came here from Chicago. I'm a bounty hunter."

"You're a cop?"

"Sort—I used to be. I'm not anymore."

"Good. I hate cops."

Maitland did not see the point in telling her that she had married one.

The woman was still looking at him. She was not drunk or high. She was gazing at him steadily, letting him know that she was looking at him and appreciating him and she didn't care if he knew it.

She said, "Do you want to go inside?"

Maitland looked back at her, no embarrassment or discomfort in his expression because it would not do at a time like this. He said, using a respectful tone, "No. I don't think so."

The woman placed her hands on the sash around her waist, let them rest there. She did not say that she had nothing on underneath, but Maitland knew that she didn't.

She said, "Don't you like me?"

"Sure. But I've got a girl back home."

"I've got a husband. In the hospital."

"I know. I put him there."

The woman did not flinch. She stood there, quiet and contemplative. After a while, she said, "I believe you."

"It was self defense. He was trying to kill, trying to murder me."

"I said I believe you."

"They're all trying to kill me. They've got the man I'm supposed to bring back to Chicago. They're going to kill him. A woman too, I think."

"And what will you do?"

"Stop them."

"Do you know where they took these people?"

"No. That's why I came here."

"You thought you'd find them here?"

"No. Well, maybe. I don't know. I thought I might find some sort of clue here."

"Instead, you found me."

"Yeah. I found you. Are you going to help me or not?"

A horn sounded and then another sound of dissonance. Chaos.

The woman gestured with her chin. "You responsible for that?"

"Yes."

"What did you do?"

"Blew up a police car."

"Nice," the woman said. "They'll be looking for you."

"I'm counting on it."

The woman frowned, confused. Maitland did not elaborate.

The woman said, "We better go inside."

This time he accepted. He believed she meant it a different way this time. And he was right.

She shut the front door when they were inside. She left the lights off.

She said, "Ted came by here earlier today. Early in his shift. This was after supper. He seemed scared, upset. And there's not much that scares him. So I figured he was in trouble at work. Criminal trouble. He was looking for the keys to a house he inherited from his family last year. He couldn't find the keys at first, so he yelled at me and accused me of hiding them. Said I'd hid them, or used the house to fuck some other guy and hadn't put them back in the right place. That's how he talks. I told him the place was a dump and I'd never go there for any reason. Of course, the keys were in the kitchen drawer where he'd left them. Under the kitchen utensils. That made him even madder, when he found them. He'd've taken it out on me if he'd had time. But he was in a hurry. He took the keys and left."

Maitland said, "Is that it?"

"That's all I know."

"Will you show me where this house is?"

"No." She said it firmly. "If they found out I helped you, they'll kill me. Or do worse things."

"They might kill this other woman too."

"That's not my problem. I'll tell you how to get there. You can even write it down if you like. But I'm not going anywhere near the place."

Maitland thought of the Gravitt girl, leading him right into the path of Ted Roke's shotgun blast. Skinny little thing with glasses, making him drop his guard. Stupid.

Maitland said, "How do I know you're not setting me up?"

The woman gave him that direct look again. Strong eyes. Finally, she said, "You don't, I guess."

Evan Maitland smiled at that woman. He even wondered, for a moment, if he should have taken her up on the offer she had made earlier. Then he thought of Julie. Julie . . . in his bed, the two symmetric valleys on her backside. He thought of Bianca teasing him about Julie, his ambivalence about her. He thought of them both, but he saw the woman in the flesh standing in front of him now.

"Well," Maitland said, "the way things are going, I'm going to have to trust someone."

The woman that was Roke's wife said, "I trust you, if that helps."

"Why? Because I almost killed the man that's been terrorizing you?"

"Maybe," she said. "But anyone could have done that. Something more. If we had time, maybe we could talk about it."

They looked at each other in the darkness. For that moment there was an intimacy between them. It was a moment he would never tell anyone about. Partly because it was his. Also, because he didn't think anyone would believe it. There was something almost unworldly about her. If there were time, maybe he could ask her where she came from and how she got to this place. If she answered, would he know her any better?

Maitland said, "But we don't—have time, do we?"

After a moment, the woman said, "You go ten miles out

194

on state road E. Turn right when you see the burned out trailer. Turn right after that. You go two miles then until you reach box 144. You got that?"

"Yes."

"If you don't find what you're looking for there, keep going. You come back here, they'll kill you."

Maitland said, "They haven't yet." He said it more for his benefit than hers. She smiled at him then and he knew he hadn't really fooled her at all.

"Well," she said, "it's better to be lucky than good."

Maitland smiled back at the woman before he left. He never saw her again.

# TWENTY-NINE

He found the husk of the burned out trailer home and turned right like the woman had told him to. Then he found box 144. Behind it was a chain link fence. There was a padlock that prevented the bar from being moved up. Maitland thought he could back up the car, get some momentum and bash through the fence and drive up the dirt path that led to the buildings. But then they would know he was coming. Behind the fence was a small white house with the windows boarded up, except one that had an air conditioning window unit sticking out. The house was dwarfed by a bigger structure behind it. Maitland presumed it was a barn.

He put the Chevy in gear and kept going.

He drove until he found a grove of trees. He parked in there and got out of the car. He took the young cop's shotgun with him. He walked, staying off the road and to the trees and whatever other cover would be available. He was scared now, more scared when he was out in the open, but it did not overwhelm him and maybe because he was frightened he let his mind rest on the woman, the cop's wife, standing on the front porch. He wondered about her, wondered if she would disappear from this world altogether. He wondered about her and it made him wonder about Julie. At first, he wasn't sure why the cop's wife made him think of Julie. One was a cop, the other a corrupt cop's wife. Why would one make him think of the other? Was it guilt? Shame for feeling attracted to the one here? Tempted by her offer? Intrigued by her boldness? The way she held her arms while she smoked a cigarette?

Maybe. But maybe it was something else. Maybe it was just survival. Need. Maybe that was the common thread. He needed the cop's wife's help and she gave it to him. When he had met Julie, he thought she was good looking. But that had been secondary. He needed her help. Men were trying to kill him and a crooked cop wanted him killed, so he asked Julie Ciskowski for her help. Asked her not because she was pretty but because he didn't know what else to do. And Julie had delivered. Julie had saved his life. After that, he became intimate with her. Which was great. He liked being with her. He liked her, maybe even loved her. Great at times, but not great at other times. Sometimes not even okay. It was during those times that he felt a tremendous guilt and shame because he resented being so indebted to her. She had saved his life, for chrissake. Can't you let her move in with you? Are you that ungrateful? He contemplated these things once in a while and felt gross. He did not have the courage or heart to discuss it with Julie. And, being a cop and an ex-cop, he had never been a firm believer in telling people everything you're feeling. In fact, he had trouble believing that people really knew what they felt anyway. Though there were rare exceptions. He remembered laughing aloud at a movie when a woman character asks her boyfriend what he's feeling and he answers, "*Fuck* is what I'm feeling." That guy knew.

And then there was Bianca. She almost certainly was aware of his ambivalence for Julie with her "maybe not" smart-ass comments. He could discuss it with Bianca. But he believed that that sort of discussion would be unfair to Julie. *See, Bianca and I were discussing this and we believe that*

. . . A surefire way to get a slap. There were already tensions on that front. Julie had come to the store once and met Bianca and Julie was struck by her beauty. And Julie was not one to be easily intimidated. Not by a damn sight. But that night, Julie said, "You didn't tell me she was beautiful." Being the fucking detective. Or being a woman. Either way, try responding to that one. Maitland did not try. He didn't say, "She's married." Because he knew that would not take care of it. He just shrugged. To his way of thinking, he had co-owned the store with Bianca before he met Julie; he did not believe he had a duty to Julie to sell out his share because of a woman's beauty.

Mead liked to give him shit about having two wives. But it was not something that Maitland found particularly funny. If there was any truth to it, it was only a matter of time before one master shoved the other off the stage.

Trudging across a cold field in Kansas, Maitland thought, what difference does it make? He'd probably never make it back to Chicago anyway. Then the two of them could fight over his CD collection.

He slowed when he saw the patrol car between the barn and the house. Another car behind it. The cop's wife had not lied to him. He felt his heartbeat. He still could not be sure. It could be a coincidence. Or it could still be a set up.

But if it was the right place, if the woman had been telling him the truth, he would have to move quickly because there was only one patrol car here now. The others were hopefully parked by the torched vehicle in town. But if they were there, they probably would not stay there all night. Damn. He had wanted to find the place, but now that he had he almost wished he hadn't.

He climbed the steel fence. Crept over to the patrol car and took cover behind it. He moved to the back of the patrol car to examine the car behind it. A Lexus. With Texas plates. Yeah, this was the place.

He looked to the house. Even smaller up close; maybe eight hundred square feet. No light coming from it. The barn behind the cars was bigger. The structure the settlers probably built first. So they were in one structure or the other. Or maybe they weren't here at all.

Ferguson looked at his watch again. It was late now and getting later. He wished they had not left him here alone. He had no one to talk to and it was hard staying awake. If he were driving now, he'd pull over and get some rest. He wished Jason and Garrett and the rest of the guys were here. Someone could relieve him and maybe he could lie down in the back seat of the patrol unit and get a nap. Or they could just get it done.

Ferguson stood and stretched. He winced when he put weight on his leg. Christ. It still hurt where the nigger had kicked him. Ted had told him nothing was broken, like he knew. Maybe not, but it still hurt. Ferguson hoped there would be an opportunity to give something back to the nigger before the night was through. A nightstick across his face maybe. He would ask Garrett when he got back.

Keep moving, Ferguson thought. Get the blood moving. Holding the shotgun to his side, he walked over to the cellar door. For a moment, he thought about shooting a blast through it. Maybe the homeboy was just on the other side of it; maybe he'd get his face taken off. But that was not what he had been told to do. Ferguson bent over and checked the padlock on the door. It was locked as he knew it would be, but it gave him something to do.

It was when he was bent over that he became aware of another person in the barn. He looked up and over to his left. There was someone there. A man pointing a shotgun at him.

Maitland said, "Put it down."

Ferguson knew that the man meant, put your shotgun down. The shotgun was still in Ferguson's right hand; he held it by the stock. His finger was not in the trigger guard. The bounty hunter was on his left . . . how? How did he get here? How did he know where to come? Christ, where was Garrett and the chief? How did Garrett let this happen? Reserve officer Larry Ferguson stood in jeans and his tan uniform top, and a man not in uniform had a shotgun leveled at him. Ferguson was still bent over. He let his fingers tighten around the stock . . .

Maitland said, "Buddy, it's late and I'm tired. You don't put that down by the time I count three, I'm going to presume you're going to try to use it and blow a hole in your fucking side." Maitland raised the shotgun. He said, "Ready to die?"

"Wait—"

"One. Two."

Ferguson dropped the shotgun on two. He stood up, his hands raised.

"Okay, okay. Don't shoot me. Please don't shoot me."

Maitland said, "Step away from it. Now."

Ferguson did so. Maitland came closer. He took in the cellar door and the padlock.

Maitland said, "Is Hicks in there?"

"Yeah."

Maitland said, "Why?"

Ferguson shrugged. Like it was something apart from him.

Maitland said, "Open it."

"I can't. I don't have the key. Ted's got it."

Maitland approached the cellar door. He said, "I don't think you're being honest with me."

Ferguson said, "This isn't my deal. I'm just taking orders."

"You're here, aren't you," Maitland said. "Get back. Further. Stop. Sit down. On the ground. Now cross your legs . . . yeah, like you're doing yoga. Put your hands on your knees. Keep them there."

Beneath the door, Nina Harrow said, "What's going on?"

"I don't know," Hicks said.

Then Hicks heard his name. He thought he'd heard the man say it before, but he could not be sure.

"Hicks! Hicks, you down there?"

Hicks said, "Who is that?"

"Maitland."

Several hours without sleep and captivity work on a person. Hicks was disoriented and not inclined to trust anyone.

Hicks said, "What are you doing here?" Suggesting he thought Maitland was part of this.

Maitland thought, Jesus Christ. He said, "I'm not with these guys, all right? They tried to kill me too."

"Why should I believe you?"

"Fuck," Maitland said. "Hicks, I don't have time for this shit. I don't have a key to this padlock, so I'm going to have to blow this door open. So step back, will you. Move." He pointed the barrel of the shotgun toward the lock. He raised his voice and said, "Clear?"

Hicks stepped back, taking Nina by the arm. He called out to the man above. "Yeah. Okay. Clear."

The blast punched a hole in the door; the padlock obliterated. Maitland pumped another round into the chamber and turned over to look at the reserve officer. He had stayed where he was supposed to.

Maitland pulled open the door.

"Come on out," he said.

Hicks came out. He saw the reserve officer sitting cross legged on the ground. Was that the one he had kicked? The man looked most unhappy. Then Hicks looked at Maitland and decided he'd have to believe he was not a part of this.

Hicks said, "Okay, Nina. Come on out."

Nina Harrow stepped up out of the hole. She looked at Maitland and the shotgun he was holding.

Hicks said, "I think he's all right. But stay with me until I'm sure."

Maitland left it alone. He nodded his head to the woman. A greeting. He felt awkward, holding the shotgun.

Hicks said, "If you on the level, you really having to work hard to make your money on this one. You think it's worth it?"

Maitland said, "I'm not sure yet."

# THIRTY

Hicks said, "All right. You got me out of the hole. But I still don't know about you either."

Nina said to Hicks: "Who is this?"

"He's the man from Chicago," Hicks said. "Handed me over to these guys."

"Hicks—" Maitland said.

"In cuffs," Hicks said. He held up the cuffs, though Nina had seen them already.

Maitland said, "You all through?" He said to the woman, "I'm a bail enforcement agent from Chicago. I came for him because he skipped town on a bond. Did he tell you that?"

"He told me." She said it in a way that let him know she trusted Hicks more than she trusted him. Well, shit.

"He told you what he was wanted—"

"He told me that too," she said, pushing Maitland back farther.

Maitland had to study her for a moment. Good-looking woman in nice clothes that were dirty now. Cosmopolitan girl. Maitland said, "Did I see you earlier today?"

"You did. Outside the police station. You got out of a Mercedes."

"Yeah," Maitland said. "It's out of commission now." He looked at Hicks, holding him partly responsible. He knew it was not rational, but it had been a long night.

Hicks said, "What did you do, wreck it?"

"No, I didn't wreck it. They shot the fucking shit out of

203

it. Let's see, this was after they tried to kill me, twice. Once at your place, another time in town. Under normal circumstances, I'd be worried about getting arrested for murder or some other crime, but these aren't normal circumstances. I'm just being hunted like an animal. Hicks," Maitland said, "what have you gotten me into?"

Hicks said, "I think you got that question backwards."

Nina said, "Be quiet, both of you." She looked at Hicks like he was slow or something. She said, "We already talked about this. It has nothing to do with either of you. It's me they're after." She looked at Maitland, gestured toward Hicks. "They just want to use him."

Maitland said, "And what did you do?"

The woman did not answer.

Hicks said, "She didn't do anything. She came up here to look for her sister."

Maitland thought of what Sadie Gravitt had told him. He said, "And that made people nervous?"

"Ah, apparently," she said. She saw the reserve officer sitting cross legged on the ground. She had not seen him before, but she could see that he was in on this. She thought about walking over and kicking in his fat face. Instead, she nodded toward him. "I'll bet he knows," she said.

Larry Ferguson saw all three of them looking at him now. Strangely, he wasn't that worried about what the white man would do. The white man was civilized; he could have shot Ferguson dead a minute ago but he didn't. But you never knew what a black guy would do. And the woman . . . Christ, they had locked her in a fucking cellar and encouraged the nigger to rape her; they had laughed about it. He would need the white man on his side if he was to survive.

Ferguson said, "I told you, I don't know anything about anything."

It was the white man who responded. He said, "I don't believe you."

*Shit.*

"I'm just—"

"You gave me a couple good kicks," Hicks said. "And then laughed with the others, telling me to rape her. Seems like you had your heart in it then. That how you treat a man? That how you treat a lady?"

Ferguson looked to Maitland. He needed a reprieve. He pointed at Hicks and said to Maitland, "Man, what are you doing? You going to believe him? He killed two people, you know he did. What are you doing?" He spoke with conviction; he sincerely could not believe Maitland was not seeing it clearly.

There was a dangerous moment then as Maitland stared at the man on the ground and entertained a very dark, violent action; a quick and sudden way to put an end to this ugliness. It would be frighteningly easy. Shoot this miserable beast now and take him off this earth. Who would blame him for doing it? But he let the occasion pass.

Then Maitland said quietly, "What are you doing? Why did you bring this man here, as opposed to a jail cell? What is this woman doing here?" Maitland looked at Nina Harrow and then back at Ferguson. "What did you do to her sister?"

"I told you, I don't know—"

Maitland fired a blast from the shotgun into the ground a few feet from Ferguson. It kicked up dirt and hay and wood splinters into the reserve officer's side and face. It took everyone by surprise. Even Hicks jumped back and looked at Maitland differently.

Maitland said, "What did they do to her sister?"

"Ahhh—"

"Answer me."

"I've got splinters in my face."

"Tell me. What did they do to her sister?"

"Christ, I wasn't there, all right! She was with Jett and Jett had done something to piss off Carl and they disappeared. That's all I know. They just disappeared."

Nina said, "Disappeared."

Ferguson said, "I didn't have anything to do with it, lady. That was Carl and Garrett's deal. I didn't have anything to do with it."

Nina said, "So she's, she's—"

"It was Garrett and Carl, lady. I swear to God I wasn't there."

Nina seemed like she was about to fall. Hicks reached out and held her arm. After a moment, she took his hand off and walked away.

Maitland watched her. Strangely, he felt his anger at the man subside. He knew the man did not deserve it, but it was not something he could help. Maitland said, "Carl's your friend?"

"I know him. He used to—"

"He's dead," Maitland said. "I killed him. I shot Roke too. You and your pals have put me in a killing mood. You want to live?"

"Yes."

"Then answer my next question truthfully. Are they planning to kill her too?"

"Yes."

Maitland gestured to Hicks. "Him too?"

"Yeah," Ferguson said. "They were going to pin it on him."

"One more question," Maitland said. "You CLEET certified?" It meant, officially trained and commissioned as a law enforcement officer.

"No," Ferguson said. "They wouldn't give me that."

"Well," Maitland said, "that's a fucking relief." Maitland turned to Hicks. "Would you do me a favor?"

"What?" Hicks said.

Maitland tossed Hicks the keys to the handcuffs. Hicks caught them.

"Will you take those handcuffs off and put them on that person. Then escort him to the bottom of that cellar?"

The meaning was not lost on Hicks. White man using the black man to belittle another white man. Well, maybe he didn't mean it like that. Maybe it was a way of saying he was sorry. Or maybe it didn't mean anything. Maybe the man was just too tired to do it himself.

Hicks said, "Don't start giving me orders."

Maitland shook his head, suppressed a smile. "I'm not," he said.

The handle was shot off, so they secured the door to the cellar by putting two heavy hay bales on top of it. Ferguson would not be able to move those.

Maitland picked up the reserve officer's shotgun and walked to where the woman was sitting. She looked up as he approached, acknowledging him. Maitland felt awkward again, standing there holding a shotgun in each hand now.

After a moment, he said, "I'm sorry."

Nina said, "I was telling Thomas earlier that I—had been thinking she was dead ever since I got to this town. You know how you sometimes feel things."

"Yeah."

"She was pretty screwed up, but she didn't deserve . . ."

"No, she didn't." Maitland said, "Neither do you."

"Why do you say that?"

"Sometimes, when something like this happens, people think they did something to deserve it. Maybe something immoral. Or something stupid. I've seen it before. When a guy gets mugged on a subway, he gets mad at himself for trying to take the train that time."

"How come?"

"I don't know, really." He said, "I just know I've seen it before." He had thought about it too; after being a police officer for a few years. He believed it had something to do with fear, and not just the fear that comes with getting the shit kicked out of you. Perhaps victims blamed themselves because it was easier to do that than acknowledge there was real evil in the world.

Nina said, "I wasn't very good to her."

"Well—"

"No, I mean, I really wasn't."

"Okay, then. Maybe you weren't. But that doesn't mean you deserve to be murdered. Any more than she did." Maitland said, "Can I get you to believe that?"

Nina Harrow looked up at this man she had met moments ago. A man who had saved her, who was now a comrade in this nightmare. It was unreal, but he had put it out there.

She said, "Why should it matter to you what I believe?"

"Because I need you." He gestured to Hicks. "Maybe he needs you too."

"You guys need me." It seemed ridiculous to her.

"If we're going to survive, yeah, I think so," Maitland said. "After it's done, after we're out of here and home safe, we don't have to talk to each other again or send each other postcards. But until we're out of this godforsaken place, I think we're going to need each other. And if part of you thinks you deserve punishment, if some good little Catholic girl in you believes you've got this coming, we're all going to suffer."

Nina looked at him for a few moments, her gaze steady and strong. Holding that expression, she said, "I think you misunderstand me."

Maitland liked that; not so much what she said, but the firm way she said it. "Good," he said. Like it settled something between them. He looked around the barn, then back to the woman. He said. "That Lexus outside, does it belong to you?"

"I didn't drive here. They kidnapped me."

"It's got Texas plates."

"Then it's mine. I guess they brought it here."

"We'll need it to get out of here," Maitland said. "The car I brought is stolen."

"You said they destroyed yours?"

"Yes."

"Why?"

"I don't know."

When he said that, Nina began to think he was okay again. She said, "It's a strange place, isn't it?"

"Yeah, very strange."

"Well," she said, "I'm not altogether sure I like you very much. But I am grateful to you for saving us."

Maitland said, "We're not out yet."

Hicks walked up.

He said, "We ready to go?" His eyes were on the shotguns in Maitland's hands; Maitland noticed it and stepped back. A reaction. Hicks noticed it, but didn't seem offended. "Yeah," Maitland said. And they started moving.

They walked out of the barn. Nina first, then Hicks, Maitland last. Then they heard something: tires scrunching, a car's engine. Engines. Two cars approaching. Nina said, "Oh, no." And as Maitland came full out of the barn he saw the two patrol cars driving toward them. Then the spotlight came on and they were in its beam, like players in a circus.

The cars stopped and Maitland knew what would happen next. He called out, "Hicks!" And Hicks turned as Maitland tossed him one of the shotguns and Maitland said, "Get her in the house! Go!"

Nina and Hicks ran, Hicks pushing Nina with one hand, hurrying her and the men in the patrol cars were out now, getting behind their doors to level service weapons. They shot first, but in the same crack Maitland leveled the shotgun back and let out a blast without really aiming it. He ran and shot off another blast at waist level. He ran past the Lexus and toward the house and he was scared almost senseless but some part of him was aware that he was in the dark, they had not moved the spotlight on him and the distance was closing and then he saw Hicks standing in the doorway holding the shotgun, looked at Hicks' expression for some sign of humanity, watched as Hicks leaned to his own left and pointed the shotgun toward the patrol cars and pulled the trigger and Maitland got to the door as Hicks stepped back in the house and shut the door after they were both in.

They paused in the darkness, shaking with fear and adrenalin, but conscious enough to wait and see if anyone would try to rush in after them so they could have something to shoot at.

There was a moment of silence.

Then the window in the room exploded.

They got down on the ground.

More gunfire poured in the window, thacking holes into the walls and refrigerator and table and chairs. It kept coming. Maitland fired a round back out the window. Then another. He looked up at the ceiling light that Nina had turned on and said, "Jesus." Then aimed the shotgun at it and blew it apart.

Then it was dark.

Maitland said, "Get in the next room. Find the woman and stay with her. Turn off every fucking light in this house. Go."

Maitland fired one more shot out the window, letting them know what would happen to the first man that tried to climb through that window. They fired back a few more rounds.

Then it stopped.

Silence. Maitland could smell the gunpowder in the darkness, feel the smoke in the cold air. He crawled through the kitchen doorway into the living room.

# THIRTY-ONE

They gathered behind the chief's car. Garrett, Bender, and Russell. Their clips and barrels were empty. Their hands shook as they reloaded and considered where they were.

Garrett said, "He's here. Goddammit, he's here."

"Why?" Russell said. "What is he doing here?"

"Never mind what," Garrett said. "How? How the hell did he know to come here?"

Bender said, "He said Ted told him."

Garrett sighed. Like he was not surprised. He said, "Did he kill Ferguson too?"

"I don't know," Bender said. "Russell. Go to the barn. See if he's in there. If he's dead, leave him and come back here. Go."

Russell hesitated, thinking of the shotgun blasts coming out of the window of the house. Bender noticed it and said, "Go *around*, Russell. That way. Go."

Russell went, doing a wide arc around structures until he got to the front of the barn.

Russell came back a few minutes later with Larry Ferguson. He was alive, but he didn't look good. Beat up and scared. He looked like he'd cut himself shaving.

Wood said, "What happened?" Not showing any sympathy when he asked.

Ferguson said, "The motherfucker snuck up on me."

Garrett Wood said, "Christ. You were probably asleep."

"No, Garrett. I swear."

"Save it," Bender said. He did not want any quarrelling

212

because they would need every available man, including Larry. He said to Larry, "Did they take your shotgun?"

"Yeah." Ferguson said, "The bounty hunter brought his own shotgun with him."

Bender said, "So now they've got two."

Ferguson shrugged. Like it was not his fault.

Bender took a breath. He did not want to hit Larry. He needed the man here.

But God almighty, he thought. Two shotguns. And the bounty hunter had shown he knew how to use it.

They sat in the darkness in the middle of the house. In the living room. The carpet was old and crusty and it smelled of mold. There was a window at the front of the house that they looked up at from time to time, like a vampire might float in front of it at any moment and they would have to shoot it.

Maitland said to Hicks, "They bring you in here earlier?"

"Not me," Hicks said. "They took me directly to the cellar in the barn."

Maitland turned to the woman. "How about you?" he said.

"No," she said. "Or if they did, I don't remember it. They used chloroform on me. I woke up in the cellar."

So, Maitland thought. They were hiding in a house none of them were familiar with. They had come in through the back door, which led straight into the kitchen. But that would not be the only door. He could see another one—the front door—in this room. But what else?

Maitland said to Hicks, "Stay here, will you? I'm going to see how many ways there are into this place."

Maitland crept around the house, peering around corners before he rounded them. There were two bedrooms connecting to the living room that also served as the dining area. One bathroom with a window too small to allow a man to crawl through; though they could shoot through it. And there was a small utility room with a washer and dryer in it. There was a door in the utility room, leading outside.

Three doors total.

He searched every room in the house for a telephone. He did not find one.

Maitland went back to the living room.

He said to Hicks, "I need your help."

"All right."

Maitland regarded the woman. Sitting on the floor, looking up at him. He was about to say something to her, but she spoke first.

"What?" she said.

Maitland said, "There are no telephones in here. So we can't call State Police. We can't call anyone."

"You su—"

"I'm sure."

The woman took a moment to gather herself.

Then she said, "Do you have another gun?"

Strange. Maitland was about to ask her if she knew how to shoot one. He could tell her he was thinking that and they could both say, wow, freaky, but there wasn't time for that. He said, "I do. Do you know how to shoot?"

"Yes. I've shot handguns before."

Maybe he had misunderstood her. It would be nice. He took the .38 Smith and Wesson snub out of his coat pocket and handed it to her.

"This is only good for close range," he said. "So try not to waste shots."

"You mean," she said, "don't shoot it out the window at birds?"

214

Jesus, being smart alec at a time like this; slap her or kiss her. Maitland said, "Yes. Don't shoot at birds."

Hicks and Maitland went to the utility room. Together they moved the washing machine in front of the door, creaking and scratching as they shoved it into place.

Hicks said, "You want to put the refrigerator in front of the door in the kitchen?"

Maitland said that was a good idea.

It took more effort to do that. The smell of gunpowder and fear was still in the kitchen. But they walked in there anyway and kept to the sides of the room, out of range. Soon they got the refrigerator in front of the door. It was while they were moving it that Hicks started to question Maitland.

"Who was Carl?"

Maitland said, "Pardon?"

Hicks said, "You said you killed someone named Carl. Who was that?"

"He was the guy in the black T-shirt. He was at your house this evening."

"The one not wearing a uniform?"

"Yeah."

"Was he a cop?"

"None of them are cops," Maitland said. As far as he was concerned, they weren't.

Hicks said, "That what you tell yourself?"

"That's how it is," Maitland said.

"Why did you kill him?"

"He was trying to kill me."

"You said that about Ronnie too."

"That's right. I did." Again, there was no apology in Maitland's tone. He told himself he should not care what Hicks thought. But it was late and he was tired and hungry and a little raw. They got the fridge in place.

Maitland leaned against the fridge. He looked right at Hicks and said, "You got a problem?"

"No," Hicks said. "I don't have a problem. Do you?"

"Yeah, I think I do," Maitland said. "I went through a lot of shit to come back here and get you, and you're bringing up Ronnie Ellis. Something you don't know anything about. You got a reason for doing that?"

Hicks looked back at the man who was looking at him.

"No reason," he said.

Maitland said, "Let me speak plainly: if we survive this thing, I fully intend to bring you back to Chicago and collect my fee. So I don't expect you to thank me for that. But it would have been very easy for me to leave you here and make money some other way." Maitland looked around the house, the situation they were in. He said, "There are easier ways to make it than this, I assure you."

"So now I'm ungrateful."

"I don't know anything about you. The woman seems to trust you, so part of me thinks you might be all right. But then another part of me is getting pretty fucking irritated at what you're implying. Do you really believe I killed Ronnie because he was black? Some deep seated, superior white man thing?"

"I didn't say that," Hicks said.

"What are you saying?"

"I just knew him. That's all."

"No, you didn't. You knew who he was, but you didn't know him."

"Okay." Hicks raised a hand. "I'll leave it alone. But tell me this: what's the difference between you shooting these men here and me putting those men down in Chicago?"

Maitland regarded Hicks for a moment. Then he seemed

to relax. Christ, he was tired. Maitland said, "There's a big difference."

"What?"

"No one's arrested me yet."

Maitland kept a straight face while he said it. And it took Hicks a moment before he got it. Then he saw the hint of a smirk in the bounty hunter's eyes. Then Hicks laughed, barking it out. And Maitland smiled.

Nina heard them in the next room. Weirdos, she thought. Both of them. Her fate in the hands of a convict and a bounty hunter making jokes while men outside tried to kill them. She rolled her eyes and smiled and for a brief moment she stopped feeling so scared. Laughing, yes. But they were men, by God. And they were on her side.

Ferguson lowered the field glasses.

He said, "It's too dark. I can't see where they are."

They were still crouched behind the chief's car. From there they could see the back door and the door to the utility room. They did not have a clear shot to the front door, but Russell had locked the front gate at the end of the drive. If they tried to run toward the road or the gate, they could pick them off as they tried to scale the fence. Bender had sent Russell over to the other side of the house in case they tried to crawl out of the bedroom windows.

They were surrounded all right, and they would be pegged if they tried to reach the Lexus between the house and the barn.

But Jason Bender did not feel good about the situation.

The thing was, the sun would be up in a couple of hours. Morning would arrive and there would be a lot to answer for. The incinerated police car; a patrol officer in the hospital with a gunshot wound; a reserve officer killed, one that too many people in the community knew to be a crank dealer as well as the brother of the assistant chief of police; a woman from Texas missing. It was a big, big mess. People would want to know where the police chief was and what he was doing about these things. It would not be just some dumbass fire chief asking questions.

The place they were at was well out of town and the next house was at least a mile away. But there was a road out front and anyone driving by in daylight would see the police cars. *Hey. What's going on there?* Or people would drive by and hear gunshots. Or they could get a call. And they would have to send a man to answer it or explain why they hadn't.

It had to be done soon.

If he had the resources of a metropolitan police department at his disposal, he could call in a tactical team with Kevlar vests and rifles and night vision glasses. Pros, sharpshooters, marksmen. All they would need is for one of the people inside to inadvertently bob his head in one of those windows then, *poof*, watch it explode as the trigger was pulled. It would help.

Maybe. Maybe not. A lot of the metro departments would only give orders to shoot as a last resort; hostage's life clearly at stake or a police officer's.

Crouching in the cold, Jason Bender wondered if it would make any difference. If he had worked for Topeka PD or KCK or the state patrol, he would not have been in this mess in the first place. But he hadn't and now he was. To his credit, he did not try to persuade himself that he was clearly in the right and the people inside were in the wrong. The people inside were there and he was out here and that was just how it was. The people inside the house needed to die and he could not be concerned about whether or not they deserved it.

Garrett was next to him. He said, "What are we going to do, chief?"

Bender acknowledged him, feeling a partial satisfaction that Wood was trusting his judgment and looking to him for guidance.

Bender said, "You still got that MAC-10?"

"Yeah, it's in the trunk."

"Okay. I want you to get it. Go around the barn, get behind the patrol car behind the Lexus. Get down behind it and stay there. I'm going to try to talk Maitland into coming out. I'm going to tell him he can take the Lexus and go. When he comes out in the open, when he gets out of the house and starts walking toward the car, put him down."

"Ten-four," Garrett said.

"Garrett," Bender said. "Don't shoot too soon. Wait till he gets away from the door. You understand?"

"I know what I'm doing," Garrett said. He was back to sounding irritated again.

The three of them were together again, gathered in the living room, shivering in the cold. They could feel the breeze coming from the kitchen where the window had been blown out.

Hicks said, "How many men they got?"

"I don't know, really," Maitland said. "Bender, Wood, the bald guy. And they've probably let the reserve officer out of the hole. So that's four."

Nina said, "That we know of."

"Yeah," Maitland said. "That we know of."

"Assume that's all there is," Hicks said. "They can go get more."

"Yeah," Maitland said. "They can. But I'm betting they won't."

Hicks said, "Betting?"

"Okay, hoping." Maitland said, "They've got murder in

mind, not capture or arrest. I don't think they want any more witnesses."

Nina held a fist up. "That's the spirit," she said. "Think positive. Win one for the Gipper."

It was Hicks who responded. He just looked at her and said, "Nina."

Nina looked at Hicks, surprised at the sudden depth in his voice. A polite request for sympathy and understanding. On whose behalf, she wasn't sure. But she felt ashamed.

She said, "Sorry."

Maitland didn't say anything.

"HEY EVAN! YOU HEAR ME? THIS IS CHIEF BENDER. EVAN, I WANT TO SAY SOMETHING TO YOU. LISTEN TO ME. LISTEN TO REASON."

They stopped. Bender was using a bullhorn. Aiming at the open space where earlier there had been a window. They could hear him clearly.

"WE'RE NOT INTERESTED IN YOU. IT'S NOT YOU WE WANT. YOU'RE LAW ENFORCEMENT. YOU'RE A COP. YOU'RE ONE OF US, IN CASE YOU'VE FORGOTTEN. YOU HEAR? YOU HEAR WHAT I'M SAYING? I'M TELLING YOU, YOU CAN GO. JUST WALK OUT. WE'VE LEFT THE KEYS IN THE LEXUS. JUST WALK OUT, GET IN THE CAR AND LEAVE. OKAY?"

Maitland looked over to Hicks, his eyebrows raised.

"JUST GET IN THE CAR AND DRIVE AWAY. LEAVE IT BEHIND YOU. YOU HEAR ME? YOU'RE FREE TO GO, EVAN. FREE TO GO."

Maitland said to Hicks, "What do you think?"

Hicks said, "Didn't you kill his brother?"

"Not his. The assistant chief's."

"Still, very forgiving fellahs."

"Well, this is the bible belt."

Hicks said, "I think you'd get about five feet out that door."

"And if I make it to the car, you'll probably unload on me."

"Yeah, I probably would."

"That settles it then."

"Evan! Come on now. It's not your fight." Maitland called out.

"Bender! Bender!" He kept his voice loud and directed it toward the open space in the kitchen. He would not walk toward it; turn down the offer to die near the car only to be shot through the window. "How about this? You and your men get in your cars and leave. Then we'll leave. No one else dies. No one goes to jail. It's a clean slate."

"No deal, Evan. You take what we offer or you can die with them. You've got one minute to decide."

Shit. For a moment Maitland had almost convinced himself that that would work. No more killing. An end to the battle. He had hoped maybe they were tired and scared too and wanted to go home. But they weren't interested. Now he felt stupid for thinking it could be mediated, naïve for hoping. They wanted the woman dead. Or maybe it wasn't about the woman anymore. Maybe it had gone beyond that now. Maybe it was just about winning. The Yankee bounty hunter from Chicago had come to their territory and shot two of theirs. And if that wasn't enough, he had taken a side in the wrong battle. In for a penny, in for a pound.

Hicks said, "You going to answer him?"

"I have," Maitland said. He suppressed the anger he suddenly felt, put it someplace else so it wouldn't upset his concentration. He said, "They're going to make a move now."

# THIRTY-TWO

When Nina Harrow was in high school, she had gone out with a boy on the varsity football team. He had been good looking, as had she, and quite popular at school. His name was Brett and Nina was flattered that he was interested in her. After a movie, they had gone to the Pizza Inn. It was there that Brett shoved a smaller kid out of his way near the bathroom. The kid was smaller and younger than Brett and after being shoved and humiliated, the kid pushed Brett back. It didn't hurt Brett, but the smaller kid had crossed a line and that was that. Brett took the kid outside and bloodied his nose and blackened his eye and threw him on the ground.

Nina had seen fights before that; had seen kids bullied, pushed around. She had never liked seeing it. But she had never seen a bully draw blood; never heard the awful sound of a fist smack firmly against a teenager's face. It horrified and sickened her. She screamed when Brett hit the kid. And she felt unclean because, even at that age, she felt partly responsible. Maybe Brett had pounded the boy because she was there to see it; show her what he was made of. At the end of the night, she told Brett she didn't want to see him again. And he said, "Baby, you know you enjoyed it." She got out of the car without kissing him or saying goodbye, ran into the house and threw up.

Fortunately, for her, Brett took interest in another poor girl and left her alone. She had nightmares about it. She believed she had witnessed evil that night. She vowed afterwards that she would never get involved with another Brett again.

She kept that vow. But it did not really solve the problem. She had never seen Michael punch out a smaller boy. And she had hardly considered him to be a "macho" rockhead sort. But as she sat in the dark house in a Kansas field, she allowed herself to wonder if perhaps Michael was a bully too. A different kind of bully. Not one that bloodied noses, but still one that pushes people around. She remembered the time he had bawled out a hostess at a restaurant. Nina had said, "Michael." And he had backed off the poor girl. And Nina made herself forget about it. Almost. A few times after, she would wonder how he treated people when she was not around. Would he have called the young girl "stupid"? A dumb, fat little goat roper? Would he have gone to her manager and tried to get her fired?

Why had she overlooked that? That and other things she pretended not to notice. She wondered now if she had sought out Michael because he was weak. He was not strong in the way a bully was strong. Michael was weak. And she knew that about him. And he was not "evil" with a capital E. But he was of weak character and she had accepted it, gone along with it.

It was on her mind now. On her mind now even though she would rather not have been considering it. Part of her thought it was not fair to think about it, not fair to put such a burden on him. But she could not help it. The thought kept recurring: what would Michael do if he were here? What would Michael do? WWMD.

Would he have said, "Take the black man. For chrissakes, take him!"

Would he have shot the bounty hunter in the back?

Would he have left her here?

God, it was so unfair to think such things about him. He

223

was not here to defend himself. Not here to conduct himself and maybe prove that her fears were unfounded. She had never cheated on him; never even allowed herself to think about what it would be like to take another man inside her. Not since they had become involved. She had persuaded herself over the years to try to see the good in people and overlook the bad because that was the right thing to do and the proper way to live.

But she couldn't help thinking what she was thinking. WWMD.


Maitland was looking at her.

Nina looked back at him. She said, "Maybe they won't."

Maitland said, "Maybe they won't what?"

"Maybe they won't try to come in the house."

"You believe that?"

"I don't know. They know we have guns. They know you're not going to leave. Maybe they'll go away."

Maitland shook his head, like he was sad about it too. "After what we've seen?" he said. "And with what you know? They've all but admitted they killed your sister—I'm sorry, but they have. I'd like to think it was finished too, but they're not leaving until they've killed all three of us."

She said, "But they're police officers."

Maitland shook his head. She of all people should know better, but she wanted to believe it was not as bad as it was. "No," Maitland said, "not really. They left that behind some time ago. Probably long before you came to town."

Nina said, "Chief Bender called you a law enforcement officer. But you're not a police officer, are you?"

"No. I used to be."

"In Chicago?"

"Yes. In Chicago."

"You don't look like one."

He had heard it before and he assumed it to be true. It was why they had assigned him to work narcotics. With his blond hair, they said he looked like your typical California surfer-dude asshole. Of course, he had been younger then.

Nina said, "You kind of act like one, though."

"You mean that in a good way, or bad way?"

"A good way." She half smiled. "I think."

"Okay."

"The way you talked to me earlier," she said. "When you said I didn't deserve this. You sounded like a policeman then."

"Yeah? I thought perhaps I'd made you angry."

"You did," she said. "But I'm past it now."

"Good," Maitland said. "If you weren't, I'd have to ask you to give me that gun back."

"Oh, you'll get it back all right." Giving him a full smile now.

"Well, at least wait until my back is turned."

"I'll do that," she said. Her expression changed and for a moment she had to struggle to hold on to her composure. She said, "I—I don't think I know your name."

"It's Evan."

"Evan. I like that name. I'm Nina."

"I know."

"Do you have a family, Evan?"

"No. I meant to, but—no. You?"

"No. I meant to, too."

"You will," Maitland said. "Help me with this couch, will you?"

Nina Harrow gathered herself and said, "Sure."

They moved the couch in front of the front door, blocking ingress. When they were done, Maitland pointed to that part of the wall that was between the two bedroom doors. He said, "I want you to sit on the floor there. Stay down. Keep that gun with you. Thomas and I are going to be at the east side of the house. Now if someone tries to come in through these windows, you let us know. If there's time. If there's not time, you kill him. If you can't do that, tell me right now."

Nina said, "I can do it."

Maitland went to Hicks. He said, "I've checked this shotgun, and between you and me I've only got four rounds left. How about you?"

Hicks said, "I've got seven."

"Well," Maitland said, "She's got five shots in the Smith and Wesson and I've got more rounds for that in my pocket."

"For a two-inch snubnose gun. We're not going to be able to use that for these."

"I know that," Maitland said. "All right. It just means we can't waste shots. No more firing out the window just to scare 'em or cure the boredom."

"Daylight's coming," Hicks said. "They're going to want to finish this before the sun comes up."

"You said that before," Maitland said. "How is it you know that?"

"Well, think about it," Hicks said. "Like you said earlier about them not wanting more witnesses around. They're going to want to get this done at night. I would if I were them." Hicks looked at him, a slight smile on his face. "What, did you think it was some sort of black extra sensory perception?"

"Yeah. That's exactly what I thought."

It was quiet out there. And the silence made them nervous. It told them that the men outside were thinking about what to do next.

Hicks said, "If we survive this, are you really going

to take me back to Chicago?"

"Yes."

"Even after this?"

"Yes." Maitland looked at the man and shook his head. Maitland said, "I'm not going to lie to you. Not at a time like this. I need your help. And you need mine. We start lying to each other and it's just a matter of time before you put that shotgun on me."

"Is it for the money?"

"Of course it's for the money," Maitland said. "But there's more to it than that. For what it's worth, I never let a skipper go. I can't. I start doing that, I just as well hand you over to the men outside."

"I don't understand that."

"I'm not asking you to understand it," Maitland said. "You know, I talked with your lawyer. He's quite put out with you."

"Ain't that a bitch."

"Goddammit, what's the matter with you? You *want* to go back? You *want* to fucking lose? The man wants to help you. What I'm saying is, he's pissed off because he thinks he can get you acquitted."

"He wants to be on television."

"He seemed all right to me. Besides, what if he does just want to get on television? If you get acquitted, what difference does it make?"

"I suppose it doesn't make a difference. If I'm acquitted. But it ain't gonna go that way. I'll be convicted and he'll still be on television."

"I'll testify for you," Maitland said.

"What can you testify to?"

"What you did here. What you did for the woman. What you did for me."

"And what is it I did for you?"

"You didn't blow my fucking head off when you could've."

Hicks remembered the frightened look on Maitland's face when he pointed the shotgun out the back door before turning it on the men behind the patrol car.

"Okay," Hicks said. "Suppose that's evidence of my good Christian nature. How is that going to be relevant to what happened in Chicago?"

"It may not be," Maitland said. "See how your lawyer can use it. Back in Chicago, was it self defense?"

"You the judge now?"

Maitland shook his head. "Right now, it makes no difference to me one way or the other."

"Why ask then?"

"I met your friend Dreamer. I got the feeling he set you up."

"I already knew that."

Maitland considered that statement. If Hicks already knew and he had not done anything about it, had not killed Dreamer . . . maybe he was innocent. Could it be that that was the real reason Sam Stillman was pissed off? He had that rare criminal defense case where the client was actually innocent? That rare Atticus Finch career moment that all but the most cynical lawyers hope for: the opportunity to defend someone that was not guilty?

Maitland said, "Was Dreamer there when it happened?"

" 'Course he was there."

"Why don't you have him testify then?"

Hicks laughed. "Man, you got a lot to learn about people. I known Dreamer since we were kids, and he set me up to be *murdered*. What makes you think he's going to get on the stand to help me?"

"I don't know. Maybe we can figure something out. A way to leverage him."

Hicks' expression hardened. "I see," he said. "You and the other noble white man going to help me out. Then maybe you won't feel so bad about taking me in, huh?"

Maitland shook his head again.

"That's not what I meant," he said. He was not going to say any more about it.

Bender gave up after twenty minutes and called them back in. They crouched behind the car again.

Chief Bender said, "Well, I guess he's not coming out."

"No," Garrett said. A hint of insubordination in his tone. "He didn't believe you."

Bender said, "You seemed to think it was an okay idea before."

Garrett Wood was aware of Russell and Larry there, waiting for his reaction. Waiting for somebody to tell them what to do.

"Okay, chief. It wasn't a bad idea. It just didn't work, okay?"

"You got something better?"

"Well," Garrett said. "How about this? We deliver fire in the kitchen and the side. Two of us. They'll fire back. Unless they took extra rounds, they can't have much left. While we're doing that, one of us goes around the back with the MAC, climbs in the bedroom window. Another one of us comes in from the front. They'll be occupied. Maybe even out of ammo. We take them from behind."

Bender said, "And who comes in from behind, with the MAC?"

"Me," Wood said. "I got something I want to say to Maitland. We let Russell go through the front. You and

Ferguson maintain a steady fire into the kitchen."

It pushed Chief Bender back, Wood offering this idea. It was not bad. For the limited resources at hand, and the time they had to operate in, it was not bad.

Larry said, "Why don't we just burn them out? Set the place on fire. If they try to come out, we shoot 'em."

"Negative," Bender said. "We don't have any gasoline here. There isn't time to run into town and get it. And even if—there isn't time for that, Larry." Bender looked to Garrett, surprised that he was volunteering to do this. "You think it'll work?"

Garrett held up the MAC-10. "This's got a twenty round clip. I can kill 'em all in one burst. They don't stand a chance."

"All right," Bender said. "We do it your way. Wait for us to start firing."

Maitland could feel the exhaustion in his fingertips. He knew they were all tired and hungry. If the men outside were smart, they would just wait for the three of them to faint. Come in and kill them while they were asleep. If he and Hicks didn't kill each other first. They were beat to shit and they would not be able to last another twenty-four hours. It was too much. And not just physically. He had come to this town about twelve hours ago. Shortly before dinnertime. The scene at Hicks' house, the running through the field, hiding on top of a grain elevator, shooting two men. Any one of those things would have exhausted him emotionally and had him begging for a nap afterward. But it just kept coming. It just kept coming and you couldn't think about how awful or frightening it was because if you did you would be defeated. You would lay down and shut your eyes and wait for them to kill you. The men outside could send someone for food and water and maybe some electric fucking blankets while they just sat inside this cold house and waited for the next commercial.

He remembered being at a scene when he was a patrolman where a man inside was holding his ex-wife and child hostage. The man was armed with a pistol and there were about eighty cops outside and a lieutenant on a telephone trying to talk him into coming out. The tact team was there, of course. The negotiator kept talking and talking and eventually the man inside lost his concentration and walked in front of a window. He was killed instantly by a sniper's bullet.

The cops cheered, not so quietly. Maitland had cheered himself. As far as he saw it, it was one turd down and the lives of a woman and child saved.

Maitland was not cheerful about it now. No, what he remembered was how long it took the man inside to get killed. It was a little under two hours. The man inside had not closed his eyes, he had merely lost his concentration and drifted in front of a window. An easy thing to do, even if you're not a turd holding your ex-wife and child at gunpoint. Few men can be expected to concentrate for that long.

Maitland said to Hicks, "Listen."

"Yeah?"

"I think I'm going to have to go out there."

"Go out there? For what?"

"To kill them," Maitland said. "Get it done before they do it to us."

Hicks stared at him. "Man," he said, "you're not thinking."

"No, listen. Maybe there's a way I can get up on the roof. They're not looking, I can take maybe two or three of them out before they know I'm there."

"That's crazy. Evan, you—you can't do that."

"Hicks, we don't have a choice. They storm us, we're in trouble. They leave us alone, we're going to pass out from sheer exhaustion."

"You still—"

Gunfire exploded in through the kitchen window.

Then more.

It came in that open space. Blast after blast. They could hear it rapping against the walls. It was terrifying and there was nothing to do but hear it.

Hicks said, "They're coming."

Maitland yelled to Nina, "Stay there!"

While one officer fired into the open space, another had driven one of the patrol cars up closer to the house. Maitland shot a round out to the windshield. But it did not stop it. The car was close to them now and he could see at least two men behind it; they had adequate and closer cover now.

Hicks shot and shot again at the car, keeping the men on the other side. He hoped he had hit at least one of them, but he couldn't tell.

Maitland shouted, "Keep them there!" Then he ran out of the kitchen.

"Hey!" Hicks shouted. But Maitland was gone.

Maitland went back through the living room. Nina was sitting on the floor where he had told her to sit. "Stay there," he said again. Then he ran into the utility room.

From behind the house, Garrett Wood listened to the gunfire. He counted to five then started to move forward. He knew he should crawl toward it, but he didn't feel there was time for that. So he half ran the distance with his back hunched over. He heard the shotguns blasting from the other side of the house and he thought that the best thing was just to get to the back of the house as soon as possible. It would be over soon, he told himself. He would kill the black guy and the bounty hunter himself. They would not see it coming, the pieces of shit. And if he were lucky, maybe the shithead bounty hunter would still be kicking out some breath while on his back and Garrett could give him another burst in his face. Say, "This is for Carl, you sack of shit." Or, "You should have stayed in Chicago, pussy." He was proud of it already; aware that Russell and Larry looked at him in a way they did not look at Jason. He was the real leader, the true chief of this outfit. Jason was just an administrator.

He reached the back of the house and crouched behind the window. Then he slowly rose up and looked inside. Good. The bedroom door was closed. He removed a slim-jim from his coat and put it in the crack at the bottom of the window. He applied leverage and got it open about four inches. Then he put his hand in and opened it further. And it was enlarged enough for him to get in. He looked to his left and right. No one outside; he was still alone. He lifted one leg into the window, then he had one foot on the bedroom floor, straddling the sill. Almost in the room now.

The door opened and he saw a form standing in the doorway. The woman.

There was a second when they looked at each other. The MAC-10 was in Garrett's right hand, but he had put the left side of his body through the window first. He began to swing it around when the woman raised her arm and fired a pistol at him.

The first shot took him in the side of his chest. Nina fired again, moved closer. Then fired again. And Garrett was punched back and out the window. She saw him buck at two of the shots, but it was happening so fast.

She hurried to the window. Against every rational instinct she ran to the window. The man had a weapon of some sort and she wanted to make sure he did not come back in again. She got to the window and looked out and saw him lying on the ground. The machine gun lay next to him. Out of his hand, but he was reaching for it, stretching his arm out. Nina Harrow shot him in the face.

Maitland pulled the washing machine back from the door so he could open it. He had two rounds left in the shotgun. Then he was outside. To his right, about forty feet, was the patrol car, the chief and Ferguson shooting over the roof with their sidearms. Maitland was out now, totally exposed.

But they did not see him. They were concentrating on the kitchen window where, hopefully, they believed he still was. There was not much there to hit, unless he wanted to go further out from the house, which would really put him out in the open. If they fired on him now, he might have time to get back in the house. From where he was now, he might be able to get a piece of Ferguson's shoulder and side. Maitland raised the shotgun.

Then heard shots coming from behind him. His heart jumped as he turned and looked around the north side of the house, where the front door was.

It was the bald cop, holding his pistol up and shooting into the front window. Maitland heard it shatter. He thought, *Nina*. Pointed the shotgun at the bald guy and fired. He saw the bald man flinch, but he did not go down. Maitland fired again and this time saw the man leave the ground, shoulders flown back like he had run into a clothesline. Then down.

That was all that was left in the shotgun, so Maitland ran toward the bald man, rounding the corner of the house as he heard gunfire behind him.

Bender heard the shotgun blast to his right and turned to see Maitland fire another one. At Russell, he thought. He's shooting Russell. He raised a bit, but then went back down as a shotgun blast came from the kitchen. Then another, the people inside the house telling him to stay where he was.

Bender said to Ferguson, "Go get him."

Ferguson said, "Are you fucking insane? I'm not leaving this car with that motherfucker blasting out the window!"

Bender's heart thudded. Because it occurred to him for the first time that in using the patrol car as a barricade, they were now imprisoned by it. Pinned here by the very people they intended to kill. They could not leave.

He waited for the sound of the machine gun.

Hicks heard the gunfire from behind him. Three shots. Then a fourth.

He shouted out, "Nina! Nina! Are you all right!"

"I'm okay, Thomas! I'm okay!"

They continued shouting at each other, each of them only catching snippets of what the other was saying in the chaos.

"What happened?"

"I just killed one of them."

"You—what! Just—get down! Get down!"

Hicks had two shots left.

Maitland ran in panic toward the bald cop, thinking, he's got a gun and I don't and I've got to get to him before he uses it. But he got there and the guy was a mess, the upper part of his body blown apart by the shotgun blast. He was dead. Maitland held his lunch and bent over and took the man's pistol away from him. It was a .357 semiautomatic.

Maitland ran back to the front of the house; avoiding the front window so Nina, if she was alive, wouldn't accidentally shoot him. He remembered that he only saw two men in front of the police car by the kitchen. The bald one made three . . . Christ, there would be another one in the back. He stayed to the side of the house and edged back to the western side. Closer, then closer to the corner. He did the policeman's quick head peek around the corner and thought he saw a man lying on the ground. Then looked again. It was a man on the ground, lying there with a machine gun next to him. Maitland held the pistol on him as he approached. He drew closer and saw that Garrett Wood was dead.

*What was Garrett doing?*

Mr. fucking strategist with his great plans. They were stuck here by these people firing from the kitchen window. They could not move. And Garrett had not done anything. Where was he? Had he run off? Where the fuck was he? He was the one that got them all into this stupid, stupid mess. And where was the bounty hunter? Larry next to him, looking like a zombie with little red cuts in his face. He said they were splinters from when the bounty hunter had shot at him. But wouldn't he be dead if the bounty hunter had shot at him? Larry disobeying his orders now. A punk, low-ass reserve officer asking him if he was insane. He should screw his Glock in the man's ear right now and repeat the order; pull the trigger if the man hesitated. But some part of him knew he would never do that because then he would be stuck behind this damn police car by himself as shotgun blasts continued to bark out of the kitchen window. He should have known not to listen to Garrett. He should have known the man was not really a police officer; just a crook with a badge. A dilettante. Garrett knew nothing of tactical operations, nothing of the buttwork of law enforcement. He was just a smiling good old boy turd that wore a uniform. And he had let Garrett come into his life and bring his dirt into the department and ruin everything he had ever worked for. Garrett and his turd brother that was thankfully dead now. He should have never taken the money from them. He should have arrested them both years ago. He should have left Union City.

The hood on the patrol car bucked as machine gun fire tore into it, shattering the headlights and windshield. The stream of bullets climbing slowly as they blew apart the red and white lights on top.

Then it stopped.

A moment later, Ferguson stopped screaming.

Maitland kept behind the corner of the house, to Bender's left. The front of the MAC-10 pointing at them.

Maitland said, "Come on out, Jason. It's over now."

After a moment, he heard Bender call out.

"Garrett! Garrett!"

"He's dead, Jason," Maitland said. "The other one too. I'm sorry."

"You killed him!"

"I'm not a killer. If I were, I wouldn't hesitate for a second to kill you now. God knows you've given me plenty of cause." Maitland said, "It's *over*, Jason. Throw down your gun and step out."

Maitland was ready. He was ready, by God. Ready enough that it scared him. If either one of those men had stepped from behind that car with anything remotely black or silver in their hand he would have emptied the clip.

But somehow they knew that. Or they had had enough themselves. They stepped out from behind the patrol car, unarmed, their hands raised.

But Bender could not face him with complete humility. It was too much to bear. He said to Maitland, "I should have taken you this afternoon."

"Yeah," Maitland said, "you probably should have."

# PART 4
## SATURDAY

# THIRTY-THREE

By nine A.M. it seemed about half the population of western Kansas was there. The fire department, Kansas Bureau of Investigation (KBI), FBI, State Police (who Maitland had called first), even a couple of detectives from Hutchinson PD; they had a file on Carl Wood and were looking for an opportunity to expand it or close it. News media too; a station from Hutchinson and a couple of vans from Wichita. People angry and people sympathetic. Everyone curious. But by noon, the fire chief of Union City had shaken Maitland's hand and told him to call if he needed anything.

Barney Withers said, "I grew up here. It's really not a bad place. There are good people here." He seemed genuinely anguished by what had happened. He looked off to the prairie like he was about to weep. He said, "Kansas has a violent history; law enforcement and lawbreakers. I wonder sometimes if the ghosts come back for more bloodshed; like they didn't get enough when they were here the first time."

Maitland thought it had more to do with crank and greed than history. But this was the man's home and he was trying to say he was sorry for something he had no part in.

Maitland said, "It's just something that happened."

"No," the man said, "it's something we let happen." He composed himself. "But maybe we can start again. Clean things up. Maybe you'll come back here and visit sometime. Under different circumstances, I mean."

Maitland nodded toward a couple of KBI agents. "I may

have to, if I can't talk these guys into getting additional statements over the phone."

"They seem to think you're all right," Barney Withers said. "We all knew the Wood Brothers, you see."

Maitland said, "I wish I hadn't."

Maitland would later wonder if the old man had a point about the ghosts. He had to return months after to testify at a trial against Jason Bender and after he had done so, could not leave soon enough. After that, it would be years before he considered even driving near the state again.

She answered the phone on the fourth ring. She said, "Oh, hi. How's it going?"

It occurred to Maitland that he had spoken to her only yesterday. A little over thirty-six hours earlier. He should not have been surprised by her relative nonchalance. She could not have known the years he had lived in that time.

"Well, I'm alive," he said. He had not meant to sound like he was bragging or seeking attention. But it was what he felt and it just came out.

"Well, yeah," Julie said. "Wait a minute; did you have a car wreck or something? Are you all right?"

"I'm fine," he said. "It got a little hairy down here. The car is totaled, though."

He heard Julie sigh. "God. Did that skipper try to shoot you?"

"No, he's all right. He's a pretty good man actually. I think he's innocent."

"Evan, why do you think that? Because he told you?"

She was a cop, he remembered. Well, he had been one too. At one time. And when he was, like just about every cop he joked about the prisons being filled with innocent men.

"It's a long story," he said. "I'll tell you about it when I get home."

"Oh," Julie said. "I thought you were just going to call me when you got home."

"Oh, Christ, woman. I want you in my home. Don't you understand that by now?"

"Well, I don't know," Julie said. "Sometimes you don't speak very clearly." She paused. "Are you all right?"

"I'm fine. I'm good, actually. I miss you."

"You miss me?" Julie laughed. "Maybe you should go to Kansas more often."

Maitland said, "No, I don't think so."

# THIRTY-FOUR

Nina Harrow insisted on driving them to Topeka, where they would catch a train to Chicago. But she got tired around Salina. So they stopped and let her sleep in the back. Hicks drove and Maitland rode next to him. Maitland spent close to an hour on his cell phone, talking to Bianca for a little while, and Charlie Mead for a longer time. He only told Bianca that it had been "pretty rough" and he would see her the day after tomorrow. And even with that, he could practically hear her shaking her head over the phone.

They heard Nina cry before she finally went to sleep. She had not done it since they left Union City, had not allowed herself to do it.

Hicks said, "She'll be all right."

"You think?" Maitland said. "She lost her sister."

"I know. But she's a tough lady."

"Well, she killed the man responsible for it. Maybe there's something in that."

"Yeah," Hicks said. "For us. We'd be dead now if she hadn't. But I don't know that it's going to bring her any peace."

Maitland didn't say anything.

Hicks said, "Something bothers me."

"What's that?"

Hicks turned around to make sure Nina was still asleep. She was. He said, "She doesn't know where her sister is. I mean, where they buried her."

"Yeah?" Maitland was not sure he understood.

"She needs to know that," Hicks said. "So she can bring her home for a proper burial. She needs to know that."

Maitland said, "I don't think anyone knows anymore. I don't think Bender killed her sister. Not directly. I think it was just the Woods. And they can't tell her where her sister's buried."

"No," Hicks said. "It's just wrong, that's all."

"Well, like you said, she's pretty tough."

The terrain became less flat as they drove further east. More bluffs, more green. Maitland felt the knot in his stomach unwind. A little.

Hicks said, "You still think you're taking me back?"

"Yeah." Maitland said, "I'm not going to chase you a second time. Costs too much. Besides, I still got the .38."

Hicks said, "I think the woman handles it better than you."

Nina Harrow cried at the train station. She cried for her sister. She cried because she was afraid. She cried because she had been through something awful. And she cried because she was grateful. Grateful to the men that had saved her life. She would not acknowledge her own part in it.

She kissed them both on the cheek. After she kissed Maitland, she clutched the front of his coat.

She said, "If he gets convicted, I'm holding you responsible."

Maitland pictured the dead man next to the machine gun. He thought about making a joke, but decided not to. He said, "I'll keep that in mind."

"You better," she said.

She hugged them both again.

Hicks was uncomfortable. He was not an effusive man.

He liked women, but would not feel even remotely comfortable demonstrating his charm to Nina Harrow. He had gotten to know her under certain conditions and there was no changing that. The woman saving their lives, then crying because she needed to cry. But he felt the need to tell her something.

"Hey," Hicks said to her and she looked at him. "You were good back there."

She smiled through her tear stained face. She seemed uncomfortable.

"I was scared," she said.

"No," Hicks said. "You were good. Remember that."

Nina Harrow watched the train leave the station. She would see them again at Jason Bender's trial, after Thomas Hicks was himself acquitted. But after that, she would not see them again. Though she would think about both of them the rest of her life.

In the parking lot of the Topeka train station, she put her head on the steering wheel of her car. She did not cry then. She simply rested it there for a moment with her eyes shut. She would need to drive straight to the nicest hotel she could find, get a shower and sleep. In the morning, keep going east to Kansas City. Then take Missouri roads down to Oklahoma, then back to Dallas. No more of Kansas, thank you.

There was so much to process, so much to think about. The ending of her engagement with Michael. A two-week leave of absence from her job, at least. A long conversation with her mother; see if things could be mended between them. And if they could not, she would have to survive that too.

She started the car and drove to the nearest Westin.

# ABOUT THE AUTHOR

JAMES PATRICK HUNT was born in Surrey, England, in 1964. In 1972, he and his family relocated to Ponca City, Oklahoma. He graduated from Saint Louis University in 1986 with a degree in aerospace engineering, and from Marquette University Law School in 1992. He is the author of *Maitland*.